ALSO BY JIM LEHRER

Viva Max!
We Were Dreamers
Kick the Can
Crown Oklahoma
The Sooner Spy
Lost and Found
Short List
A Bus of My Own
Blue Hearts
Fine Lines
The Last Debate
White Widow
Purple Dots
The Special Prisoner
No Certain Rest
Flying Crows
The Franklin Affair
The Phony Marine
Eureka
Mack to the Rescue
Super

Oh, Johnny

OH, JOHNNY

A NOVEL

Jim Lehrer

RANDOM HOUSE
TRADE PAPERBACKS
NEW YORK

Oh, Johnny is a work of fiction. Though some characters, incidents, and dialogues
are based on the historical record, the work as a whole
is a product of the author's imagination.

2010 Random House Trade Paperback Edition

Published in the United States by Random House Trade Paperbacks,
an imprint of The Random House Publishing Group,
a division of Random House, Inc., New York.

RANDOM HOUSE TRADE PAPERBACKS and colophon
are trademarks of Random House, Inc.

Originally published in hardcover in the United States by Random House,
an imprint of The Random House Publishing Group,
a division of Random House, Inc., in 2006.

LIBRARY OF CONGRESS CATALOGING-IN-PUBLICATION DATA
Lehrer, James
Oh, Johnny: a novel / Jim Lehrer.
p. cm.
ISBN: 978-0-8129-7944-2
1. Marines—Fiction. 2. Baseball players—Fiction. 3. First loves—Fiction.
4. World War, 1939–1945—Pacific Area—Fiction. 5. Combat—Psychological
aspects—Fiction. 6. Homecoming—Fiction. 7. Life-change
events—Fiction. I. Title.
PS3562.E4419038 2009   813'.54—dc22   2008016563

Printed in the United States of America

www.atrandom.com

2 4 6 8 9 7 5 3 1

Book design by Victoria Wong

To Bob Loomis

Oh, Johnny

JOHNNY WRIGLEY THOUGHT he felt slight lurches and heard braking screeches, among other signs that it must be slowing down again. But after five days and four nights in the confining world of this slow, crowded troop train, he was beyond recognizing much of anything. All he knew for sure was that he was one of several hundred brand-new, gung ho United States marines on the way from South Carolina to California and then on to some island in the Pacific where he was going to kill Japs for America.

"Listen up!"

He and the fifty other marines in his railroad car went quiet and looked toward a tall, portly army sergeant at the south end of the car, the direction the train was moving—more or less.

"We're in Kansas, the Sunflower State!" barked the sergeant.

All Johnny really knew about Kansas was that his baseball hero and center fielder role model, Pete Reiser, was playing for an army base semi-pro team called Fort Riley somewhere here

· 3 ·

in Kansas. Many of the pros were playing ball for the war effort.

"Feel welcome and be happy!" the sergeant said.

The marines' word on the army sergeant was that he had been assigned to permanent troop train escort duty because he was too old and fat for combat. His voice was perfect for this kind of thing. It was pure bellow.

There were whistles, cheers, grunts, groans, and yeahs from the troops after the sergeant's announcement.

Johnny didn't know about the welcome part, but happy, yes, he was happy. At least, considering where he was and where he was going—and why. There was a kind of happy excitement from the special camaraderie of being a United States marine on a train going someplace far away with so many guys like him, all ready and eager to do whatever it took to win the war against an enemy of evil slant-eyed monsters.

Johnny was also happy because he was beginning to get the hang of how to chew tobacco—how to stand the awful taste, and the nastiness of spitting the juice out and away far enough to keep from getting it on himself or anyone else. He'd been working on it as best he could, mostly during stops and out open windows when the train slowed down. Since boarding the troop train, so far he'd bought two pouches of Red Man, the baseball players' favorite. Almost all pro ballplayers chewed Red Man, Johnny knew from the sports pages. It went with batting and catching. Johnny Wrigley would chew Red Man when he became a pro ballplayer.

Baseball was the real happiness of Johnny's life and future. The Class B Detroit Tigers farm club over at Shepstown, just seventeen miles east of his little western Maryland hometown of Lafayette, had told Johnny to come for a tryout the day he graduated from high school. Shepstown was a city of thirty-two thousand, according to what they said in the 1940 census, compared to around twenty-five hundred in Lafayette.

Johnny was a center fielder with an aggressiveness and an arm so strong, said the Tigers' scout, that he reminded the scout of Pete Reiser. That was the ultimate thing anybody could have said to Johnny. Pistol Pete, as they called him, was the star center fielder for the Brooklyn Dodgers. The nickname came from his going after fly balls like a bullet fired by a pistol, sometimes so fast and ferociously that he banged into walls.

Kansas? As far as Johnny knew, Maryland, where he had lived all eighteen years of his life so far, didn't even have a nickname. But here he was in the Sunflower State. Last night in Saint Louis it had been Missouri, the Show-Me State, as announced by the sergeant. Before that had come the Hoosier State of Indiana, and before that was Ohio, whose nickname Johnny couldn't remember. All of the states went vaguely into Johnny's mind as more entries on the list of exotic, unknown places he had been to for the first time ever since he'd ridden the Blue Ridge Motor Coaches bus into Baltimore to join the marines. Playing pro ball was not possible now because most minor leagues had or were going to shut down for the war.

"We're about to make a stop at a place called Wichita," said the sergeant. "You can get off the train, stretch your legs . . ."

His voice was drowned out by the roar of cheers.

"We'll be here twenty-five, maybe thirty minutes . . ."

More cheers.

"Ladies will be present at train side . . ."

Whistles and hoots.

". . . to hand out apples and cigarettes."

More cheers.

"Watch your mouths, manners, and hands."

There was a smattering of "Aye, ayes."

"The MPs will be out there watching."

Now there was no question the train was slowing down. Johnny, sitting in a window seat, looked out at what there was to see of Wichita, Kansas. The outskirts, at least.

There was a huge grain elevator as big as many office buildings in Baltimore, small but neat white houses, and blacktop roads with a few cars. It reminded him of the West Virginia panhandle not far from where he lived. He had a feeling you could see across Kansas all the way to California, it was so flat. Except for the mountains. The Rockies were out there in the West somewhere.

"You been laid yet?" asked the marine sitting next to him.

Johnny only shrugged, keeping his eyes on what he could see of Wichita, Kansas, his mouth chewing on a gob of Red Man.

He had exchanged only a few words with this guy since the

guy had swapped seats so Johnny's original seatmate could join a hearts game several rows back. All Johnny knew about the new kid was that his name was Darwin and he was from a town in Mississippi—not that far from New Orleans. There was no urgency to find out more. There were still days to go before they got to California—and beyond.

"No girl's going to put her mouth on yours if it's full of that god-awful tobacco crap," said Darwin.

"Girls love ballplayers," said Johnny with a lot more bravado than his experience warranted. "Chewing's part of what they love."

Darwin shook his head in a sign of disbelief. "Chew all you want, but what I'm saying is that this might be our last chance to get laid before some Jap blows us to smithereens," said Darwin, who smiled and then gave a shrugging laugh. Most everyone from the recruiting office to boot camp who talked about dying did so with a shrugging laugh. Even Johnny.

Because of what Darwin had said, Johnny's thoughts now were about how awful it would be to die without ever having gotten . . . well, you know, gone all the way with a girl.

Gotten laid. That was what Darwin had said. Johnny had heard it called that before, but he had never actually said it. He had no idea where the expression really came from except that you had to lie down to go all the way with a girl.

THE TRAIN WAS almost at a full stop. It had been pulled by a Seaboard Coast Line Railroad engine when they'd started off in South Carolina, and it had been picked up in relay fashion by the Pennsylvania and other railroads along the way. Now, as Johnny had seen during a brief middle-of-the-night pause in Kansas City, it was the Santa Fe's turn. He believed—and felt—that this somehow had transformed the entire train, made it different. This was a new train, not the same one he'd been on for so many days and nights. It didn't make sense, but it made him feel good.

"Remember—only thirty minutes!" yelled the sergeant. "You hear a long whistle from this train, you get your butts back on here. Do you hear me?"

"Yes, sir!" came a shout from the troops.

"A second whistle means the train's moving. A third means you missed it, you're a wartime deserter, and the MPs take you in irons to another place in Kansas—Leavenworth. You're put up against a wall in front of a firing squad. Do you hear me?"

Again, Johnny and the other marines bellowed back loud and clear. Marine DIs loved to scare recruits with talk of a big federal prison at Leavenworth where there were firing squads.

Johnny and Darwin were on their feet, out into the aisle, and ready to make their way quickly to the doorway as soon as the train stopped.

Johnny leaned down to keep his eyes on Wichita out the windows. They were downtown; the train tracks were elevated. He saw that this was more than just a place. It was a real city with tall buildings off into the distance—buildings as big as the grain elevators he'd seen earlier. There was a hotel down there on a wide main street, wider than most he had ever seen anywhere else—even in Baltimore. He could read the big sign. EATON HOTEL.

"I heard about a corporal who could do it in seven minutes," said Darwin, who was gangly and tall. He had crew cut hair that appeared to be almost black. All heads had been cleanly cut at Parris Island before the troops had boarded the train.

"Do what?" asked Johnny, but he knew the answer. Everybody knew what *it* was.

It was getting laid. There were several marines in boot camp who talked about *it* day and night—on marches, before taps, at reveille, at chow, before inspections, after inspections, at the rifle range. *It, it, it.* Doing *it,* getting *it,* smelling *it,* finding *it,* lucking into *it,* getting *it* free, paying for *it,* imagining *it. It. It* was what made the minds of some of these young marines go round and round. Back home in Lafayette, Maryland, none of Johnny's friends had done *it,* but they had all talked about *it.* Kissing two girls more than once closed-mouthed on the lips and putting a hand on the butt of one of them for a count of ten was as close to doing *it* as Johnny had ever gotten.

"There are no happy dead virgins," said Darwin.

Johnny did know about virgins. They were women who had not yet done *it,* including Jesus' mother, who had had her baby while still being a virgin. Johnny knew that only because he'd heard it talked about the few times he'd gone to a Methodist Sunday school class, which he had had to do in order to be eligible to play on the church's softball team one year with his best friend, Mickey Allen, whose dad was the preacher and coach. For sure, Mickey had never done *it*.

Johnny's mom, Sylvia Alice Wrigley, worked overtime most weekends as the manager at the town's only seven-days-a-week grocery store. She had had to work hard like that since her husband—Johnny's daddy, Jack Wrigley—had run away on a merchant marine ship from the port of Baltimore and drowned somewhere. Good riddance, Sylvia always said, and Johnny, who was seven when Jack disappeared, always agreed. Johnny had only vague memories of his father or even what he looked like. But occasionally in high school Johnny had looked over into the stands from center field or from his batting position at home plate and seen the face of a guy he'd thought for a flash might be his father.

Johnny figured that his mother would organize some kind of funeral service—maybe even at the Methodist church—for her son, Johnny, if he died in the marines. But what if they couldn't find the smithereens that were left of him? How many pieces of a dead marine does an undertaker have to have for there to be a funeral? Mickey Allen, whose preacher dad had had to go to a lot of funerals, had promised Johnny that he would make sure his friend got a full-treatment marine funeral if and when it became necessary. As it turned out, Mickey had gotten there first. He'd joined the army instead of the marines and been killed in a bombing raid in France. Mickey's infantry outfit had been mistakenly hit by some U.S. Eighth Air Force B-17s in what somebody said was called a "friendly fire" incident. Johnny had already been in boot camp at Parris Island when it had happened, so he hadn't been able to attend Mickey's funeral and find out how much of Mickey had been left for a funeral.

Never mind about that kind of stuff, thought Johnny. Americans are supposed to do the killing; Japs and Nazis do the dying.

The alive marines in front of them now were shoving slowly toward the exit at the end of the troop car. The thirty minutes were ticking away. That was what Johnny was really concerned about, but, to make conversation, he said to Darwin: "What exactly are you talking about?"

"You and I die virgins, we die unhappy, Wrigley. That's what I'm saying to you. That's all."

"Aren't all virgins women?"

"Only half of 'em are."

They finally got to the vestibule for the steps down to the station platform.

Johnny looked out. There were marines in all directions. There were also at least two dozen civilian women holding white baskets of apples and cigarettes. A few looked as young as Johnny. One over there in particular was a looker. A *real* one. One really beautiful girl.

He couldn't remember ever seeing a more beautiful one.

It was as if there was a soft spotlight of some kind on only her. Just on her, like she was a star at a theater or at a circus.

She seemed frightened. There was so much noise, confusion. There were so many of those grinning marines moving around, smoking, laughing. He watched her. Occasionally a marine reached into her basket for a pack of smokes. Nobody took an apple.

Johnny saw her looking right at him. They were only forty feet apart. He was still standing up there on the railroad car steps waiting his turn to jump off.

Out of the crowd of marines, she was looking only at him.

And Johnny saw only her. She was the most beautiful girl he had ever seen in his life. *Here I come, Oh, Johnny, Oh,* he wanted to yell to her.

"Oh, Johnny! Oh, Johnny! Oh!" was a song his mom had sung and hummed to Johnny when he was a little boy, particularly at bedtime. She'd said it was a World War One ditty, but it talked about a soldier named Johnny who could really love and make a sad heart jump with joy. Out of embarrassment, Johnny finally made her quit doing the song when he got older. His dad had never sung nor hummed, but before he disappeared, he did become the first person in the world to put a baseball in Johnny's right hand. The feel of that hard white ball with red seams had been part of his life ever since. For several years, as a kid, Johnny went to sleep most nights holding a baseball wrapped tightly in his fingers. As long as he could hold a baseball, everything would be just fine.

Johnny had a dream in high school that a man, dripping wet and holding a shark under his arm, came down from the stands at the ballpark, yelled that he was Johnny's "proud pop," and gave Johnny a thumbs-up and a pat on the back for a great catch against the fence at center. Johnny responded by whacking Jack Wrigley across the side of the head with a bat. Johnny loved the sound of that bat cracking against the wet skull and then watched with pleasure as the head and the rest of Jack Wrigley disappeared over the fence in center field. Johnny wasn't sure if it was a nightmare, but whatever it was, he never told his mother or anybody else about it. Not even Mickey.

Now Johnny was afraid the beautiful Kansas girl wouldn't be able to see his head above the other marines once he was on the platform. He wasn't that tall—five feet and ten and a half inches, which, according to the newspaper sports pages, was also Pete Reiser's exact height. Pete, at one hundred and eighty-five, outweighed Johnny by five pounds. Johnny's hair was dark brown but mostly invisible, of course, because of his marine haircut. He had freckles on his face, one of the major things besides baseball that he remembered inheriting from his runaway father. The guy in the dream who'd said he was Johnny's "proud pop" definitely had freckles, but that was because his mom and others in the family always told him that Jack Wrigley was freckle-faced. Could this beautiful girl see freckles from this far?

Johnny reached into his mouth, grabbed the mess of Red Man, and tossed it straight down onto the ground and away.

Then, after wiping his mouth with the back of his hand, he stepped down. Johnny could still see her. The imaginary spotlight was still shining on her. She was just standing there in the middle of everything. Alone, not moving. Like she was paralyzed, lost. There was something about her that he had never seen in a girl before. Beyond just being gorgeous. But what? And how could he tell much of anything from this distance? Except that her skin was silky. Was she wearing any makeup? It sure did look like it, or else her face was just naturally rosy. Her hair? Like silk, too. A lightish red-blond. She had curly bangs that seemed to float down her forehead. The hair itself was almost to her shoulders but turned up at the edges. Like a movie star's. Her dress, blue with tiny yellow flowers, was up to the top of her neck, but short-sleeved. Her arms were like those of a fairy princess.

He pushed his way through. Now here he was, standing right in front of her.

"Hi," he said.

"Hi," she said.

She was about five feet four inches tall—half a foot shorter than him. He looked down at her. She smiled. It was the most spectacular smile on the most spectacular face he had ever seen.

He knew she could see his blue eyes, which his mom had always said were a knockout. And the freckles all over his face, particularly on his nose and forehead—maybe not so impressive. But maybe she'd noticed the substantial muscles in his shoulders and arms.

"Would you like an apple and some cigarettes?" she said, pushing a white wicker basket toward him.

Her eyes were dark brown, almost black. That reddish blond hair, with those perfect bangs, gently curled like feathery down from a pillow. And, yes, there was some makeup, maybe a brush of powder and a touch of lipstick. Her dress went down to below her knees, but he could see enough of her legs to recognize perfection. Betty Grable's legs weren't any better than this girl's!

She was art. Johnny Wrigley hadn't looked at a lot of paintings. But this person—all of this girl—belonged in a frame. She was a creation as much as a human being. She was *art*!

He let his eyes leave her just long enough to reach a hand to the basket and grab a pack of Camels.

"You ought to take an apple, too," she said. "An apple a day keeps the doctor away."

"Where I'm going there's no way to keep the doctor away," he said.

The words probably came over as phony posing, which was what they mostly were. He hoped he sounded exactly the way a U.S. marine—a leatherneck, a real hero on the way to war, or Randolph Scott playing one in a movie—ought to talk to a beautiful girl.

"God will protect you," she said.

He loved the sound of her voice. Soft enough to soothe but loud enough to hear, it reminded him of a woman he'd heard on the radio. She also sang. He couldn't remember her name, but it would come to him.

"You sound like a movie star," he said. "You know, one of the actresses or singers."

"I don't go to movies—none of us do," the girl responded.

"None of us what?" Johnny had no idea what she meant.

"Randallites," she said. "We're Randallites."

Johnny still didn't know what she was talking about and didn't really care. He tossed his head playfully to the left and to the right, as he always did before making a throw from the outfield, and then reached into the basket again. He hoped she believed there just couldn't be a man or boy in Kansas who looked or moved like him—not at this exact moment. He suddenly felt powerful, sure of himself. He was Johnny Wrigley, center fielder and marine.

"Yellow apples like these give you a stomachache," he said, holding an apple in his right hand with his fingers like it was a baseball. "My mom works at a grocery store and she sells them only for cooking. We only eat the red ones, mostly the Delicious kind that grow all over where I live."

"We eat both the red and the yellow," she said. "I never heard of anybody in Kansas getting a stomachache from eating a yellow."

"Here's what they're really only good for," he said.

He drew his right arm far behind him, leaned back, and then thrust forward with all the force he could muster.

He assumed the beautiful girl felt the wind from his moving arm and then watched in awe as that yellow apple shot into the air and sailed up, up, and away, disappearing off in the direction of downtown Wichita and the Eaton Hotel.

"Who did that?" some marine yelled. "They're saying that apple hit a car down there."

Several of the marines around Johnny reflexively moved away, but a couple continued staring right at him.

"The MPs are coming this way," one of them said to Johnny. "You better get lost quick, Marine."

"Is there anywhere around here I can hide for a minute?" he said to the beautiful girl.

"Follow me," she said, as if it were a completely natural thing to say.

"I'm Johnny," he said. "I'm a ballplayer."

"My name is . . . Betsy," she said. "I like to sing."

" 'Haunted Heart' is my favorite song," he said.

"My favorite is the hymn 'Rock of Ages.' "

"I like 'Bringing in the Sheaves.' "

"I read a lot," she said.

"I like mostly the O. Henry stories—you know, the surprise-endings ones," Johnny said.

"What *I* know is that the stories that matter the most are in the Bible," she said as she led him down a ramp away from the railroad platform as if it were a completely natural thing to do.

JOHNNY SHUT THE door behind them. There was no electric light on in the room, but sunlight coming through two high windows made it possible to see what the place was all about.

There were at least thirty cardboard boxes printed with CAMEL, CHESTERFIELD, or LUCKY STRIKE and almost as many bushel baskets full of yellow apples. Shoved together off to one side were also an old wooden desk with a chair behind it, a small blackboard mounted on an easel, and a brown canvas cot.

Johnny figured this might have been a railway mail room before the troop train ladies took it over as a storeroom.

"This is you-all's CP, right?" he said to Betsy.

She clearly didn't know that CP was marine talk for "command post." She just nodded.

"Wow," he said, looking around. "I've never seen so many smokes and yellow apples in my life."

It seemed such an unimportant point to make when his

mind was brimming with thoughts about what was happening right then.

The beautiful girl Betsy and the freckle-faced marine Johnny were facing each other right in the middle of it all, less than three feet apart.

"Thanks for saving me," he said. "The whistle hasn't blown and I haven't missed the train, but they might have shot me at Leavenworth anyhow—you know, for the apple."

He could see she didn't know exactly what that meant, but she said, "You're welcome. It was probably the wrong thing for me to do, though."

"I won't tell anybody."

There, written in neat printing on the blackboard, was today's date in April 1944. And under that was a list of several female names.

"Your duty roster?" he asked, pointing toward it.

"No . . . no," she said. "I'm a Betsy."

Johnny saw no Betsys on the blackboard. But it was just a quick glance.

He stepped over to one of the Camels boxes, ripped open the top, and took out an entire carton of cigarettes containing twenty packs.

"Don't do that," she said sternly. "Its a sin to steal."

"Okay," he said, and put the carton back into the box. "I'm sorry."

"Jesus said it's a sin to smoke as well as to steal, you know," she said.

"I'll have to take your word for that," he said. "I don't re-member anything Jesus said about smoking Camels. I'm work-ing on being a chewer more than a smoker anyhow."

The beautiful girl frowned, and she pinched her nose with her fingers. Johnny so much wanted to move her hand from her nose and gently touch her soft bangs, toss them aside and then watch them come back to place. And say he was so sorry that just the mention of his chewing tobacco had made her frown.

"Jesus speaks to everyone, even to those who do not . . . well, practice their faiths in a formal and regular way," she said. "We are all children of God."

She was clearly trying her best to sound sincere. He figured this Betsy the Beautiful was probably not keen on people like him who were not even close to being regular churchgoers—going to a Methodist Sunday school for softball reasons didn't count—but there was a war on and she was patriotic. And here he was a hero marine on his way to fight for America.

"What brand of church are you?" Johnny asked, wishing im-mediately that he hadn't said "brand," as if talking about Luck-ies or Camels. "Denomination" would have been better.

"I told you I'm a Randallite," she said, as if announcing the Second Coming of Jesus himself. "We follow the teachings of Heinrich Randall, who was persecuted as a heretic by the Lutherans and the Catholics in Europe for supporting a church of believers rather than a state-run church. He believed in adult baptism only instead of infant baptism and in—"

Johnny stopped her with a shake of his head. He didn't want to hear any more about churches, most particularly about anybody named Heinrich or what he believed about anything.

But she wasn't finished. Betsy the Beautiful only paused for a breath and said, again as if speaking the word of the Lord: "We believe that no man should ever take up arms against another. When God said 'Thou shalt not kill,' he meant in war, too."

Johnny knew about some Amish and other Mennonite people who felt the same way about war and killing. There were several living in small settlements north of Lafayette and in Pennsylvania near Hanover and York. Johnny saw them around in their horse and buggies, simple clothes, and long beards. They mostly sold produce at street markets and otherwise kept to themselves.

"Some of our men refuse to go to war," she went on. "Those who do go work as ambulance drivers, chaplains—not real soldiers. My uncle is with the army in France right now as a medic. . . ."

Johnny started shivering—shaking. He wasn't really cold. How could he be? This was a warm spring day and the room was almost hot, made more so, it seemed, by the strange odors—and this magnificent girl. Maybe he was sick? Scared? Or maybe just excited? Johnny didn't know himself.

"I'm not a medic," he said, folding his arms across his chest. "I'm one of those who might have to be helped by one . . . someday—someday soon, even."

Johnny felt Betsy suddenly wanted to hold on to him.

Maybe he imagined that. He must have. But he felt the sensation of a big magnet pulling her toward him like maybe he was the silver dollar his high school coach had given him for hitting two consecutive homers in a regional championship game against Frederick.

She said, "God has a plan for each of us. You can't know his plan for you."

"Yeah, I can. I've already dreamt a hundred times about it happening."

She said she didn't want to hear his dream. But it was her turn to listen, whether she wanted to or not.

"I'm in a foxhole with another guy. I'm down in it like this."

Johnny stepped over to the cot and lay down, faceup with his arms folded across his chest. He closed his eyes.

"We're talking baseball, the other marine and me, maybe about how the Yankees will probably take the Cardinals or the Dodgers in the World Series like they always do. You follow baseball?"

Betsy said no. She spoke softly.

"Baseball against your religion, too—like war and the movies?" he asked, almost in a whisper. "Baseball's going to be my life . . . after the war's over."

"I'd like to spend my life in music, singing mostly. I don't pay that much attention to any sports. A few of our Randallite boys play them, though. Jesus doesn't mind as long as the desire to win doesn't become so important that it causes sinful actions. . . ."

Johnny was still on his dying dream.

"I hear a motory whine noise overhead. Somebody yells 'incoming,' and the next thing I know, I look down at my head that is right there in my hand. Not a scratch on it. Not even any blood. It was just blown off, right into my mitt . . . you know, like I had my baseball mitt on my hand and instead of a baseball, I caught my head. Then I stick the head back on my neck like nothing happened. Like I caught a fly ball and threw it back to the pitcher."

Betsy moved to the cot, went to her knees beside it—him.

"Open your eyes so you won't see it anymore," she said.

He turned his body toward her, looked at her. His blue eyes were full of tears. "I'm scared." That's why he'd been shivering.

"I know."

"Marines aren't supposed to be scared."

"Everybody gets scared."

"How do you know that?"

"It's in the Bible."

"I don't know much of what's in the Bible."

"That's all I know."

He turned away from her. He started shaking again.

Without a word she climbed onto the cot and lay down next to him. She reached across his chest with her right arm as he turned to her and then pulled her to him.

He quit shaking.

Their cheeks were hard against each other. So were their bodies.

He stank of sweat and chewing tobacco. And he so wished he didn't.

Johnny was taking huge breaths of her. Perfume, soap—maybe with a touch of dust. It was magic. He felt like he was somewhere else.

"All I know about dying in war is what I learned in boot camp, war movies, and at Antietam," he whispered into her ear.

"Is Antietam in the Pacific?"

"Antietam's a creek in Maryland, my state. We went over there to swim and fish, except when the water rose and rushed after the snows melted in the spring. They fought a big battle in the Civil War all around the creek at Sharpsburg, only fifteen miles from my town. It was the bloodiest day ever in an American war—at least, up till now. They'll probably beat it by the time this one's over. Nearly twenty-six thousand Yanks and rebels were killed or wounded that day. We went over there one day on a school trip. There was a park ranger guy who told us every bloody detail of what happened. It was truly awful. Guys—some younger than me, even—blowing each other's heads and arms and legs off. Sticking bayonets through each other's stomachs. There was a slide show of some pictures taken on the battlefield. Dead bodies stacked on top of each other. They said they were the first real battlefield photographs ever. There's no telling how many there will be from this war."

"All war is bad," she said. "They shouldn't take pictures of it."

"You don't need pictures," Johnny said. "The park ranger let us read several of the letters the soldiers from both sides wrote home after Antietam."

And as he spoke, the full realization of what he was doing hit him. For the first time in his life, he was pressing his body hard against a girl's. For the first time in his life, he was in bed with a girl. Even if it was on some old cot, he was actually lying down with her. And she was a lovely, beautiful, nice girl. Religious, too.

She was the most magnificent person he had ever known, much less touched.

"How old are you?" he asked. "Are you still in high school?"

"I'm about to graduate," she said. "I'm seventeen."

"Me, too. I'll be eighteen next month."

"That's good."

"Why is that good?"

She didn't answer him, probably because she didn't know why she'd said that was good.

He knew it was good because an almost-eighteen-year-old marine from Maryland was holding on to the most beautiful girl of his life for dear life. For dear life. Yes, for dear life.

And she didn't seem to mind.

She didn't seem to mind when he raised his head back, brushed back her bangs, looked into her eyes. But she frowned again when he kissed her on the lips.

But she seemed all right again when he then ran his hands down her body, pulled up the skirt on her yellow and blue flowered dress, and gently rolled her underneath him.

He could feel her body fluctuating wildly with spasms of red-hot flashes, which he assumed were from the raging fires in hell, where they were both probably headed. Or maybe not.

Johnny was going to explode—into a whole different kind of smithereens. He had had several wet dreams, but the build-ups, which he could always barely remember afterward, had been nothing like this. One or two guys in high school had said they had jacked off after intentionally daydreaming about a particular girl, and so had a few marines in boot camp. He'd done something like that a time or two himself. But right now what he was feeling seemed brand-new—and unbelievably wonderful.

Spectacularly wonderful. Wonderfully spectacular.

"I love you," he said to Betsy the Beautiful.

"Don't lie—that's a sin, too," she said. "Just do whatever you do."

"I've never done it before. Have you?"

"No," she snapped. "Certainly not!"

Johnny kissed her again—quickly. He was afraid he had made her mad. And maybe ruined everything.

"My aunt Lena, she's the one married to my medic uncle. She's done it before with him—her husband. She says it all comes natural."

"An old guy down the street said the same thing to me once. So did some of the marines. But I figure most of them don't know any more than I do. I don't know what 'natural' means."

"I don't either, really," said the girl Betsy.

She moved her head upward, closed her eyes, and mumbled, "Forgive me, Father, for the mortal sin that is in my most evil heart and soul at this very moment. . . ."

And the room shook from the booming sound of the troop train's whistle. The time was up.

Without another word, he did what came naturally.

So did she.

Only barely. And the result came after only a few seconds, as the train whistle sounded again.

Betsy the Beautiful began crying. She did her frantic best to straighten herself, at least physically, using the long skirt of her dress to wipe her eyes—and the rest of her face.

Johnny jumped up and over her to the storeroom floor.

Tears still coming, she did not look at herself down there as she pulled up her white cotton panties, which, Johnny could tell, were sopping wet. With *what*? Blood? Urine? Or something else? Maybe something that had come out of *him*?

"I love you. I really do love you—please don't cry," he said as he feverishly zipped up his pants and straightened his khaki-brown uniform shirt and tie.

Betsy turned away from him. "You don't love me," she sobbed. "You don't know a thing about me."

He said, "I know you better than anybody I will ever know in my whole life."

"I have sinned, I have sinned, I have sinned," the girl said over her sobs.

Johnny had a quick stupid thought about an O. Henry surprise-ending story, and maybe here he was living in one with this beautiful girl Betsy coming from out of nowhere in a nowhere place named after the sunflower.

The ending right now had to be his getting back on that troop train.

"I hate that taste in your mouth," said the beautiful Betsy, no longer sobbing.

"I know. I'm sorry, and I promise I'll never chew tobacco again," Johnny said as he raced through the door, running as fast as he ever had.

IN SEVERAL GIANT strides, he was at the top of the station ramp.

The troop train's whistle sounded for what he knew was the third and last time.

Two MPs were standing on either side of the doorway to the platform. Were they going to arrest him—right now?

He could hear the sounds of the train. A squeaking, a rough and harsh chug, and then another.

Behind the MPs at the track, he could see the train beginning to move. Marines were hanging out railroad car windows exchanging waves with the hostesses who were lined up, formation style, on the otherwise now empty platform.

One of the MPs jerked his head toward the departing train. "Go, go, Marine—if you can catch it."

Johnny took off running like he was going for a fly ball in

deep center field that could end the game—*the* game. Several marines were standing in the vestibules of the cars, leaning out, ready to help him scramble aboard.

Johnny, still running at full speed, reached out both hands and was pulled up, up, and away.

JOHNNY MOVED THROUGH the crowded aisles to his seat, which was in the third car from the front on the fourteen-car troop train. But he was really no longer on that train. He remained in those precious minutes with that beautiful girl. No matter what might happen later in the war, he had had a lifetime of paradise on that Kansas afternoon.

For however long he lived, he would always—*always*—be in that storeroom with that beautiful girl named Betsy.

He hated it that she'd been crying when he'd left. Somebody—one of the guys at Parris Island—had said real virgins cry like hell the first time they do *it*. And they bleed like hell because some kind of thing breaks down there in them. It hurts like hell. That's what the guy had said. That's why they cry. This girl had been crying like she was hurt.

Was she worried about getting pregnant? No way that could be. They weren't in there . . . you know, together doing *it*, long enough for that. It couldn't have been more than a minute or two—maybe three. Doesn't it take longer than a minute or two to get that kind of thing done? Exactly how long *does* it take?

Johnny so wanted her to have enjoyed doing *it*—short a time as it had taken—as much as he had. He didn't want her to feel bad about what she had let him do. She had no need to ask forgiveness for anything. She wasn't a bad person. She was a glorious person. She was the most spectacular person he had ever known. She was a princess—a queen, a star. He hoped she didn't cry for long. And wasn't really hurt. Or if she was hurt, he hoped it didn't last. If there was blood, then there was probably some on him, too. But if there's no blood, that means she wasn't a virgin? No, no, no. She was definitely a virgin as well as a princess, a queen, and a star. He'd look later at what was on him when he got a chance to go to the head on the train. . . .

"Hey, there you are," said Darwin, the kid from Mississippi. "I thought you might be on your way to Leavenworth about now."

He stood up so Johnny could slip by to his spot in the window seat.

"What's that on you I smell?" Darwin said, pinching his nose. "Cigarettes and apples? Yeah. Man, you must have buried yourself in 'em."

Johnny smiled but didn't say anything.

"There's something else mixed up in it," Darwin said, making long sniffing sounds with his nose as he sat back down. "Perfume? You get close enough to one of those Kansas girls to get her perfume on you?"

Again Johnny said nothing.

Darwin sniffed again. "Hey, Marine, and there's something else, isn't there? I'm smelling more than perfume, smokes, and apples. Is it the stink of sex? Oh, my God, man. You couldn't have gotten laid back there. Not for the first time in your life. I can't believe it. Where did you do it? Who was the girl? I really can't believe it. What was it like? How long did it take? Seven minutes—more or less?"

Johnny just kept looking out the window at farms and flat fields, small roads and towns, the same kind of stuff there was coming into Wichita. There was more Kansas. But this time he saw nothing but paradise.

After a few minutes, with only a half turn toward Darwin, Johnny said: "That woman on the radio Saturday mornings. Her voice sounds like chocolate. She sings, too. What's her name? I can't remember it."

"You talking about Dinah Shore?"

"Yeah, that's her, I think. She sings that song, 'Haunted Heart,' doesn't she?"

"You laid Dinah Shore back at the Wichita train station? Now, I really can't believe *that*!"

Johnny Wrigley kept his eyes out on Kansas, his mind back among the smokes and the yellow apples, and his mouth opened in a smile as big and as deep as center field.

JOHNNY COULD SEE the names of some of the towns as the train occasionally slowed down to pass through them. Wellington, not even an hour away, was still in Kansas. Then came a few in Oklahoma, called the Sooner State, according to the sergeant. Alva, Waynoka, Woodward. Texas, the Lone Star State, was next. Canadian, Pampa, and, finally, Amarillo. Some of the names had some familiarity to Johnny. He had heard them in cowboy movies, which he had gone to regularly with his high school friends. Randolph Scott had been his favorite male movie star even before *To the Shores of Tripoli,* and an even newer marine movie called *Gung Ho!* had gotten him interested in being a marine. Johnny had always seen Mr. Scott as the perfect cowboy. He'd loved him in *The Desperadoes, Western Union, When the Daltons Rode,* and *Jesse James,* his all-time favorite. Didn't Jesse James do some of his robbing and killing in Kansas? Johnny wondered now as he thought about it if maybe there had been a movie starring Mr. Scott that took place in Dodge City? Wasn't it out there somewhere in Kansas? Had to be. How about Abilene? Wasn't there a movie that had a big cattle drive through the town of Abilene?

But mostly Johnny couldn't have cared less about movies or where he was now or what he was seeing—or even, now, where he was going.

He could still feel every detail. He could see her. Not her body because she'd remained pretty much fully dressed the whole time they'd been on that cot. And it had all happened so fast. But her face, those bangs, that beautiful simple honest face would be with him for the rest of his life.

He could see that face even in the train window. He thought

about what he would say if he wrote her a letter. Wouldn't that be great to write her a letter? Saying things like this?

Dear Betsy,

What kind of singing do you do? I'll bet you're good, whatever kind. Hit parade, hillbilly—church stuff, even. What about "Haunted Heart"? Do you sing that? It's about love. I heard it on the radio a few times. Betsy, I did not lie when I told you I loved you. You don't have to know anything about anybody much to fall in love with them. I swear. The exact split second I saw you on that platform, I knew you were the girl for me. What happened on the cot . . . well, that really was natural. We did it even when we didn't know our last names. You said your first name was Betsy. If your name was Suzy or Fanny . . . no, maybe not Fanny. All I'm saying is that names don't mean anything about falling in love. Nothing does. What are your favorite colors? Pink, red, blue? I don't care. Food? Are you a burger or a hot dog person? Or a cheese sandwich one, like me? Milk or orange juice? Regular mayonnaise or Miracle Whip? None of it matters. None of it. I fell. I mean, I fell in love with you like falling off a cliff. Or the side of a mountain. Or a ship. I could have known you since grade school, played tag and done multiplication tables or read O. Henry stories together. None of it would have made us fall in love. That's not the way it works. Not for me, at least.

Gradual isn't the way it happens—know you better and better and more and more a little bit at a time, then comes a moment when I love you. Not me.

The sergeant announced that they could get off the train again in Amarillo for another twenty minutes. There was joy among the troops as there had been in Wichita.

But it was almost dark, and Johnny had no desire to leave the train. He could still see her in the reflection of the window. He still had a lot to say to her, so much maybe that he would never not have enough to say in a letter.

Dear Betsy,

If what you call God's plan is for me not to die in the war, then I will come back to Kansas. It can be any kind of god you want. What did you say it was? Heinrich or something. I will find you and tell you in person that I love you. And prove it. I want to marry you. I want us to have a life together. I want us to be Mr. and Mrs. John Charles Wrigley. Call me Johnny. Oh Johnny Oh. That's what my mom calls me. You'll love meeting my mom. She works nearly every day at a grocery store. You can call me anything. But mainly call me a ballplayer. A center fielder. I'm good, and I'm going to be even better. As good as Pete. Pistol Pete Reiser. I'm sure you don't know about him, but, trust me, he's the best. . . .

Darwin got up to leave the train for the break at Amarillo.

"You're not going to try for a two-for-two?" he kidded. "Might as well put a Texas piece on that belt with that Kansas thing you got. Hey, why not, Wrigley?"

Darwin was still fishing for confirmation—for a story. Johnny had never said a word about anything that he had done with the girl in Wichita. He hadn't even really said something had happened.

Once Darwin left, Johnny checked on his own Skivvies and his privates. Everything down there was wet. It was too dark to see for sure, but he didn't actually see any blood. But it didn't matter. Betsy the Beautiful had been a virgin. He knew she had been a virgin.

And he said some more to her.

Dear Betsy,

I'm so sorry I had to run away so fast. But I would have been in real trouble if I had missed that train. Real trouble. They would have arrested me and taken me to Leavenworth as a deserter. And shot me. I mean it. They'd have done that. Marines do stuff like that. Being shot that way would have been worse than by a Jap. I mean that. Dying isn't all the same. If Robert E. Lee or McClellan or one of those other Civil War generals had shot a deserter, that would have been worse than getting it point-blank Yank to a rebel in one of those Antietam cornfields. I barely made the train. There were MPs standing there, but they gave me a chance to make a run for it. The train was already moving. I ran as fast as I ever have. You should have seen me. Someday if I really don't die and I find you, you might see me run like that in the World Series. I'm serious. I'm a real ballplayer. The Detroit Tigers offered me a contract to play with a minor league team, but the war came. I was going to be drafted, so I figured why not join the marines. Everybody says they're the best. I know what you said about not going to the movies, but that's not the same for me. To tell you the truth, I think seeing Randolph Scott play marines had something to do with my deciding to go into the marines. Most of my friends went into the army, except those who like water, and they joined the navy. My mom cried and begged me to do something else besides the marines. But I'll be back when I'm through with the Japs. Everything matters so much more to me now that I love you so much.

Then Johnny reached down inside his duffle bag in the overhead baggage rack, pulled out his toothbrush and a tube of toothpaste, and went to the lavatory at the end of the car.

He brushed his teeth and gargled for several minutes until he was sure there was no smell or taste left of any Red Man chewing tobacco.

THERE WEREN'T MANY lights to see after the train left Amarillo. They said New Mexico and then Arizona were coming up before California, which would be sometime tomorrow—whatever tomorrow was.

And then they would be assigned to units, put on ships, and sent on to the Pacific.

Darwin returned with a full report on what it was like on the platform at the Amarillo train station.

He sat down and leaned over to Johnny as if he had something top secret from a Jap spy to report. "I got laid, Wrigley, just like you did. It was really wonderful. There was this beautiful little Texas girl, all cuddly and cute. All I did was wink and tell her I was about to go on a suicide mission to kill Hirohito, and she came running. We went off into the Colored waiting room, which was empty because you don't see many marine niggers. We lay down on a wooden bench. I told my Texas girl I didn't know how to do it, but she said she'd show me. Which she did. Boy, she was good and she was quick. The whole thing, from beginning to end, didn't take more than two and a half minutes—way, way under the seven-minute rule."

And he gave Johnny a playful punch on the shoulder and laughed.

"Had you there for a minute, didn't I, Marine?"

Johnny gave him a quick made-up laugh.

He looked back out the window at the blackness of somewhere—presumably in western Texas, New Mexico, or Arizona. Soon he was again all aglow throughout himself when he saw the beautiful face of Betsy, who was a singer whose favorite song was "Haunted Heart."

Dear Betsy,

I didn't lie to you to get you to lie down with me. I really was scared. And shivering. I love you, Betsy. I love you with all of my heart—my haunted heart—and soul forever. I know it's hard to believe, but it's the truth.

"ANYBODY HERE AN athlete?"

That was the question that ended up putting a flamethrower on Johnny's back. A sergeant tossed the question out to a formation of the fresh replacements during their very first day on an island named Pavuvu, an awful mess of muck, land crabs, and rats that was being used by the First Marine Division as a staging area for the next big battle.

Johnny, in violation of the cardinal marine rule about never volunteering, shouted, "I am, Sergeant!" Johnny was actually thinking maybe the First Marine Division might be organizing a baseball team there on the island. He had instant visions of playing games against army teams with major leaguers— maybe even with Pete Reiser! Why not?

"Congratulations, Private," said the sergeant. "You're our new flamethrower man."

Within minutes, Johnny was out of that formation and in a tent gazing down on what he knew to be one of the most dangerous pieces of equipment any individual marine could ever use. He had heard stories in boot camp about how the enemies' favorite targets were flamethrower operators. The Japs'd lie in their gun emplacements or whatever, look for a signaling spurt of the liquid fire, and then open up with everything in that direction. The not so funny joke was that even second lieutenant platoon leaders had a longer life expectancy in combat than enlisted flamethrower operators.

Johnny had just come off a nearly monthlong trip in an old freighter doing double duty as a troop ship, from a port outside of Los Angeles. Johnny had wondered—only for a passing moment—if it had been a ship like this that his father had fallen off of when he'd drowned. Not that it mattered. What did matter was that the freighter was a floating hellhole in rough seas and Pavuvu, pronounced "Pah-voo-voo," was a hellhole on even rougher land. Compared to either, that troop train had been a thing of magnificent comfort and luxury.

It was while on the freighter that Johnny had written his first letter home to his mother. She had given him a small stub of a yellow pencil and several sheets of thin stationery with orders to "write me, or I'll cry mustard."

He had also decided it was time to write a real letter to his Betsy—a real Dear Betsy letter. He had a lot to say to her.

"*Dear Betsy,*" he began. And he stopped the pencil. After what seemed like forever, he finally came up with his opening lines.

"*I hope you know who I am. I'm Johnny. Johnny Oh, as my mother calls me. Her name is Sylvia.*"

The pencil then remained absolutely still. It never moved across the page again. He continued his Dear Betsy message by speaking it. He talked quietly, almost in a whisper, so no one around could hear.

He said:

To tell you the truth, I know it's stupid to try to write you a letter. I don't even know your last name or where you're from. What am I going to do, mail it to "Betsy, Kansas, USA"? I guess maybe not. But it wouldn't matter that much if you didn't get my letter. I'm just doing it so I can talk to you. I am not much of a letter writer anyhow. That's mostly because I usually don't have that much to say. But that's all different now. Because of you. I have plenty to say to you. My handwriting is not very good either. I never figured out the right way to hold a lead pencil. I know about what to do with a Louisville Slugger, all right. Whack a baseball with it from here to kingdom come. But I'm not so hot with a pencil. I stick the thing straight up and down too much between my right thumb and forefinger. My teachers always tell me to let it fall back a bit and not hold it so tight. You probably wouldn't be able to read anything I wrote. I couldn't say much anyhow about what we're doing. It's been a while since I saw you. I can say that, I'm sure. I can say that I think about you all of the time. All of the time every day and every night. I have this strange feeling that I know you better than anybody else ever in my life. Am I crazy?

He wanted to keep telling her everything he had done and was doing right now, and everything he was thinking and dreaming. But that couldn't be done. Even if he could have written well enough to do it.

He knew for censorship reasons, for instance, that he couldn't even tell Betsy, his mom, or anybody else that he was on an island somewhere in the Pacific Ocean.

And now, the fact that he was a flamethrower operator also had to be a military secret.

"WELCOME TO THE suicide squad," said a sergeant who needed a shave and a haircut—as well as a sense of humor.

There was another marine in the tent, which was large and tall enough for standing. He was a corporal who, like the sergeant, was thin and seemed worn-out.

Johnny had seen only pictures of flamethrowers in training movies. What he saw now was something with two large metal tanks mounted on a steel tubular frame, a smaller tank in the middle, with a rubber tube coming out of the bottom that was attached to a trigger and firing mechanism that resembled a small machine gun.

"All right, Wrigley, let's begin at the beginning," said the corporal, who was black-haired, dark-complexioned, and only twenty or so years old. But he seemed a hundred.

Part by part, the corporal disassembled the flamethrower and laid each piece on the ground. There were the three tanks, several valves and washers, and the various elements of the ignition system. He explained that jelled gasoline, called na-palm, was in the two larger tanks, air pressure for the firing process in the smaller one. Johnny could smell the gasoline. It was terrifying.

"There'll be another marine assigned to you as an assistant," said the corporal. "He'll carry two extra tanks of napalm, tools, yours and his rifles, and whatever else you need. He'll turn on the valves that let the juice flow whenever you're ready to fire . . . after you ignite the tool."

He said "tool" like it was a thing to fear.

"You smoke?" he asked Johnny, who nodded—fearfully. Lighting up around this flamethrower had been the furthest thing from his mind since he'd walked into the tent.

"Got a Zippo?" asked the corporal.

"Mostly I just use matches. I don't like fooling with the lighter fluid. Actually, I was chewing more than I was smok-ing. . . ." Johnny caught himself before he laughed out loud at the stupid thing he'd just said. Here he was talking about chewing and not liking to mess with lighter fluid, while learn-ing how to light up a flamethrower!

The corporal reached into a pocket, pulled out a silver cig-arette lighter, and tossed it to Johnny. "This is my present to you, Wrigley. The official fire starter gadget that goes with this thing is worthless. The lighter'll be the most important piece of gear you'll have."

The corporal and the sergeant ran Johnny through a series of drills on assembling and disassembling the flamethrower.

"Here, you go, Marine," said the sergeant finally. "Try it on for size."

Before Johnny could say anything, the contraption was lifted up onto his back like a pack, his arms stuck through straps on either side to keep it up.

Johnny had never had anything on his back heavier than this. At first he thought he couldn't hold it. That he would fall backward, or forward—or through a hole in the ground.

"Seventy pounds of hot stuff is what you've got there," said the sergeant. "Think of all the little nips you can burn to a crisp."

They made Johnny double-time nearly a mile to a firing practice area.

"Might as well get used to running with that thing on your back," said the sergeant.

"It's a lot easier than when some Jap's shooting at ya while you're movin'," said the corporal, who, somebody said, was on his way home in a few days. They said he'd been hurt, but Johnny didn't see any signs of wounds. What he shared with the sergeant besides leanness was a dark hollowness in the eyes. Johnny hadn't caught either of their names.

Johnny hoped he wouldn't look like them when the war was over.

Here he was at a large clearing in front of a small hill of hard rock. Everything on this island that he'd seen so far that was not mud seemed to be made of this kind of rock. He heard the word "coral" thrown around as a way of describing what it was. He had yet to know about coral.

The side of the hill was pockmarked with large black splotches, clearly the result of flamethrower blasts.

The corporal said, "Let's see what kind of shot you are, Wrigley."

"Point it like you would a rifle but from chest level, not up against your chin," said the sergeant. "Always fire from the kneeling position, never while standing or prone—lying down."

Johnny knew damn well that the prone position meant lying down on your stomach. It was one of the main ways to fire a rifle. . . .

The other two marines escorted Johnny to a spot at least twenty-five yards away from the hill.

Then with a prayer to God, the first of his life that he could remember, Johnny did, step by step, everything he was told to do with that flamethrower, including using the Zippo.

Johnny went to his knees, pointed the firing mechanism—the tool—toward the hill, and squeezed the trigger.

Out of the nozzle came a long heavy string of fire the scary likes of which he had never imagined possible.

He felt the kick from the shot and the heat from the fire, which crashed into the side of the hill.

And he saw an imaginary face up there ahead of him. It was that of a Jap soldier. His smiling face was burning to a crisp.

In a way that he had not expected, Johnny felt good about what he had just done. He knew he was going to be a terrific—if not great—flamethrower operator.

But what Johnny said in his Dear Betsy afterward was all about something very different.

Dear Betsy,

I've been so lucky because the marines made me a base-ball player. I know you're not a big baseball fan, but I wanted you to know that I hit a home run with two men on base to win a game for a California marines team in a game against a U.S. army air corps in Florida. I made a dream of a catch in deep center to save a run in a game the other day against a navy base, too. I know you don't know baseball, but you'd have been proud of me. I know you would have.

JOHNNY AND THE other marines practiced saying it out loud on the small transport ship the night before they went ashore.

"Pel-le-loo. Pel-le-loo."

"I think it's only right that we can pronounce the name of the place we're going to die," said a private named Anderson who had just been assigned to be Johnny's flamethrower assistant.

Peleliu, which was the way it was spelled, was where they were going ashore. Johnny figured it was probably best not to even say that out loud to Betsy.

Most of his Dear Betsys were about imaginary baseball games and heroics that never happened but that made Johnny so happy to describe. He also reported a few real things about Maryland, particularly Baltimore, which Johnny spoke passionately about, how it was about time it had a major-league team instead of one that was only in the triple-A International League. He knew Betsy didn't care anything about that, but it gave him something to talk about.

"Peleliu or Pavuvu. What's the difference?" Anderson said. "They're both little shit piles of sand and coral that nobody's ever heard of and never will."

Johnny thought there had to be at least one big difference between the two islands. There weren't any Japs on Pavuvu, and he figured there were bound to be more than a few on Peleliu.

Nobody was going to miss Pavuvu, that was for sure. Johnny heard scuttlebutt that an idiot navy admiral had picked the deserted island as a rest and preparation place because it had looked so beautiful and peaceful from his airplane. He had clearly been too far up to see the thousands of treacherous land crabs and rats, among other monstrosities, that had made it all so miserable.

The only good thing that had come from the misery was Bob Hope. Johnny did his longest Dear Betsy ever about the wonderful, wonderful man named Bob Hope and what he'd done.

In July, Mr. Hope had been with his touring USO troupe at another island sixty miles away when somebody had told him about the fifteen thousand marines waiting on an island "worse than Devil's Island" before they had to launch another invasion. Mr. Hope, according to everybody who seemed to know, had immediately changed his schedule. He and singer Frances Langford, comedian Jerry Colonna, and several others had flown in one at a time in a tiny Cub airplane that had landed on a coral road because there was no airstrip on Pavuvu.

Johnny had been there along the side of the road with thousands of other marines to cheer when each big star had arrived and departed. They'd also all roared appreciation at every joke and song during the hour-long performance.

Mr. Hope had made a joke about the Pavuvu land crabs at the expense of Bing Crosby, his friend the singer who owned several racehorses. "I noticed your sand crabs," Mr. Hope cracked. "They reminded me of Crosby's horses because they all run sideways." Johnny had never laughed so hard in his life.

Johnny swore then and there that he would never listen to anybody else's radio program or, except Randolph Scott's, go to anybody else's movies other than Bob Hope's. Johnny also, then and there, replaced Dinah Shore with Frances Langford as his favorite woman singer.

Johnny shared almost every second of what happened in a Dear Betsy, particularly about Frances Langford's singing.

He even mentioned it in a real letter to his mom.

IT WAS ONLY after Johnny and his fellow marines of the First Division were aboard ship that they were told officially that Peleliu was the destination. The scuttlebutt was that the brass expected the operation to be over in two or three days. It would be mostly a low-resistance mop-up operation after air and naval gun power had blown away the Japs on the island.

Nobody believed that, particularly the veterans of the division's earlier battles at Cape Gloucester and Guadalcanal. Those were supposed to have been easy going, too. Thousands of marines had been killed or wounded in those assaults.

"They either got no intelligence or they're liars," said Johnny's platoon sergeant, who had won the Bronze Star at Guadalcanal. "Best to always count on there being a Jap bullet on the way to your head from the second you hit the beach."

The sergeant mumbled this to another sergeant in the ship dining hall over the traditional marine pre-assault breakfast of steak and eggs. Johnny was at a table behind him and overheard it.

A guy at his own table said: "I hear Chesty told his people that he wished he had life insurance on the lot of them. He'd be a rich man after Peleliu."

That didn't make sense to Johnny. Chesty was Colonel Chesty Puller, a marine legend who had won a lot of medals for personal heroism. But Johnny had heard from Darwin, his troop train seatmate, who had been assigned to Puller's regiment, that many marines hated Chesty for measuring success in combat by how many of his marines died compared to somebody else's. That supposedly showed how tough *he* was. Bullshit.

The official word on Peleliu was that it had to be taken from the Japs to protect General MacArthur's flank when he went back to the Philippines. It was a badge of honor for marines to make obscene jokes about MacArthur and his slow-moving army forces, but none of that mattered to Johnny. The only thing he thought about besides Betsy and baseball was wanting to have a chance to show what he could do with his flamethrower.

He had gotten so good he could put a thin stream of fire in the center of a target the size of a pillbox window—or a man's head—from fifty yards.

ANDERSON, JOHNNY'S ASSISTANT flamethrower operator, didn't even make it to the beach of Peleliu, that place where he had been so sure he was going to die.

They were going down the side of the ship on a rope cargo net, taking their turns to board a mechanized landing craft below. The small boat, called an amtrack in shorthand for "amphibious tractor," was bobbing up and down in the rough water and bouncing repeatedly off the side of the larger ship. It was 0530, still dark, but Johnny and Anderson, like all marines, had been trained extensively in going down these nets, a crucial move in any amphibious operation. "Hands on the vertical, feet on the horizontal" was the training mantra for how to descend the net one careful step at a time.

Both Johnny and Anderson, beginning with their steel helmets, were so loaded down they could barely walk. On his back Johnny had a small knapsack of his personal gear strapped onto the flamethrower. Around his waist were two canteens of water and a first aid kit hooked to his cartridge belt. Anderson carried extra tanks and equipment for the flamethrower along with his personal gear on his back. He also had his and Johnny's M1 rifles, each weighing nine pounds, hanging off his shoulders.

On the order of a demarcation noncom, they slowly swung themselves over the side one leg at a time. Anderson was on Johnny's left. He was about the same size as Johnny—five feet ten inches, one hundred eighty pounds. Fairly well built. Also the same age. Probably eighteen—maybe nineteen. They had never talked about that kind of personal stuff. Who cared how old anybody was?

"Be careful now," said Anderson to Johnny.

Johnny didn't have to be told that. The net's rope was wet and slippery, and he was concentrating intensely on stepping and holding everything the right way. He also took a look straight down at the amtrack some thirty feet below. The waves were tossing the craft up and down. Johnny reminded himself of the crucial need to properly time his last steps into the boat. The worst thing was putting your legs inside as the craft was bouncing its way up. He'd heard about marines having both legs broken that way. Some had been killed. . . .

"Oh, no!"

It was Anderson.

Johnny looked over as the kid, having obviously lost his hold and his balance, was falling backward through the air, pulled straight down like a rock by his heavy load.

Johnny watched Anderson's helmet come flying off. He hit a side railing of the amtrack headfirst and then fell between the two boats just as the smaller one came smashing into the other.

By the time Johnny got down there, marines and sailors had pulled Anderson's crushed body out of the water and laid it down on the boat's bottom. They had already called for a stretcher to be lowered over the side to bring Anderson back topside.

Anderson's head was a bloody mess.. So were his legs and feet. They were twisted. Bones were sticking out from the skin. There was little about him that resembled a person, a human being.

"You want his tanks and stuff?" a corporal asked after noticing Johnny's flamethrower.

Johnny didn't answer. He couldn't. But the corporal and some other troops turned Anderson over, removed the spare tanks, and found a way to tie them onto Johnny's back.

"You want one of the rifles?" another marine asked.

Again Johnny could say nothing. But soon he had an M1 in his left hand. Johnny didn't bother to check the serial number to see if it was his or Anderson's. What did it matter?

Johnny had never seen a dead person his own age before. He'd been to a few open casket funerals, but they had all been for old people. And they had all been dressed and made up to appear alive. There was nothing about Anderson that looked alive.

Johnny, almost by duty rote, shuffled himself and his burdens over to the other side of the amtrack. Then he stuck his head over the side and threw up every bit of the United States Marine Corps' steak and eggs he'd had for breakfast.

"You okay, Marine?" said Johnny's platoon sergeant, who came up to his side. "I'll give you another assistant after we hit the beach."

Johnny didn't turn around. Or say a word.

The amtrack was chugging through the water now toward the beach.

Johnny hadn't even known Anderson's first name. Or where he'd been from. Or what he'd liked to eat. Miracle Whip or regular mayo? Or if he'd played ball. Or if he'd ever been laid. They'd never taken the time and the risk to get really acquainted. That was probably a good thing. Nobody needs to have a new friend who'd just died falling off the side of a ship.

There was terrible noise coming from in front of them. Johnny raised his head. The air was full of smoke and streaks from rocket fire and bombs. He saw a Higgins boat, another kind of landing craft, explode in the water a few yards to their left. Parts of it and the marines on board went flying into the air. Ahead he saw the burning remains of one, two, three, and maybe four other landing craft that hadn't made it to the beach. There were marines in the water everywhere, some of them trying to swim and calling for help, others floating, beyond help.

Yes, there were Japs on Peleliu—thousands of them. Maybe millions.

Johnny thought that this was going to be as bloody a day as Antietam.

And he bet real letters would be written by real soldiers and marines after Peleliu.

He so hoped there would be at least one that began, *"Dear Betsy . . ."*

JOHNNY NEVER THOUGHT much about miracles, the Bible kind he'd mostly only heard about in passing at his Methodist Sunday school. But he knew a lot about the special kind of mayonnaise called Miracle Whip, because of his mom. With her work at the grocery store, she had developed her own jokey way to communicate with her son, particularly about what he'd done in school or in a baseball game. The best of most anything was a "chocolate éclair" or an "apple pie à la mode." The worst, a "spinach sundae." A good grade in algebra—or history or chemistry—would be "a real Miracle Whip." She also called it that when Johnny got a great hit to left or made a tough catch on the run at the ankles. Not so good grades or plays were called things like "fizzing Pepsi" or "Crisco lard." There were always more Miracle Whips for Johnny's ball playing than his schoolwork, except when he said or wrote anything in English class about an O. Henry story.

Johnny's talk of apples in that train station conversation with his Betsy was a natural part of what passed for a special family language with the Wrigleys. Sylvia Wrigley called most every kind of minor ailment, from a cold to a stomachache, "a yellow apple." To Sylvia, blisters on a heel, boils on a neck, rashes on an arm, were yellow apples.

Johnny saw finding Betsy the Beautiful at the Wichita train station that April Sunday of 1944 as something much more than a kind of mayonnaise. It was a real miracle, in a league with somebody pitching a perfect game or hitting a grand-slam homer in the ninth inning of the seventh game in the World Series.

Right now, five months later, as he lay facedown behind a damaged amtrack just beyond the beach on Peleliu, he knew that being still alive was definitely another real miracle—the second biggest of his life so far, beside and along with his Betsy. It had to be. There was no other explanation.

His amtrack had made it to the beach, the front ramp had gone down, and he and the other twenty-five marines on board had run off, dodging Jap bullets and rockets and avoiding stepping on the bodies of dead and wounded marines who had landed before them.

But everyone had run off in all directions, looking for cover, not taking the time or the risk to stop long enough even to fire a shot back in the direction of the Japs. There was high ground just beyond the narrow sandy beach that looked like a mixture of green brush and rock. Johnny assumed that was where the Japs' constant rain of fire was coming from. So much for an easy mop-up operation! This was even *worse* than Antietam, it seemed to him. And he thought this directly in words he formed but never said, even in a whisper, in a Dear Betsy or a real letter to his mom. He never could or would do that. Anything like that.

Johnny had no idea where anyone from his platoon or even his company or regiment was. The flamethrower was still on his back. But he had yet to use it against a Jap. And now, amidst the beachhead and perimeter sounds of shots, booms, and screams, he considered ending his heroic new career as a flamethrower operator. Why not? He had no assistant to turn on the tank valves. The sergeant who'd promised to get him a replacement for Anderson had been hit in the chest within seconds after they'd left the amtrack. Johnny also realized in this horrific chaos that there were dangers beyond being a target after firing the flamethrower. Any second now a stray bullet could hit those tanks of napalm on his back and he would be a burst—and then toast.

His—or maybe it had really been Anderson's—M1 rifle was there beside him. Johnny could ditch the flamethrower and rechristen himself as a simple rifleman, try to find his or some other outfit and at least maybe prolong his life awhile. . . .

"Hey, Marine!" said a slurring voice above him. "I need your fire machine! The fire-ah! Come wishth me!"

Johnny turned around and looked up. There was a marine armed only with a .45 pistol. That marked him as being an officer because they mostly carried only sidearms. In keeping with combat procedure, there were no rank insignias on his fatigues—marines called them utilities. There was something different about him. He seemed so sad. There was a glassy look in his eyes. And he kept shaking his head as if to clear it out.

"I don't have an assistant operator, sir," said Johnny. "He died."

"I know what to do with a flamethrower. Get your assh in gear—now. I said now. Get your assh up here now. Do it now."

"Aye, aye, sir," said Johnny, thinking this guy must have taken some kind of jarring. Maybe a grenade or artillery shell or bomb had exploded near him.

Johnny, though, felt a surge of excitement. *I'm more than just a rifleman. I'm a flamethrower operator, the best in the goddamn marine corps, and here I come, you little yellow apple slant-eyed Crisco lards!*

Johnny took off in a slow, crouched jog behind the other marine, who, after a stagger or two, ran fairly straight and at a good pace.

They moved for several minutes amidst the commotion, the whizzing of rifle and machine-gun fire.

On the other's signal, Johnny jumped into a large hole that probably had been created earlier by some kind of bomb or artillery round. It was deep enough to protect Johnny and the other marine.

"Right ahead up there . . . directly ahead of us . . . maybe sixty yards away, there's a Jap machine gun . . . a rocket launcher and God knows how many riflemen inside a concrete bunker," said the marine. He was talking a little better. "They've got my platoon down. Down, down, down. We can't move."

So, thought Johnny, this poor guy was definitely an officer. A platoon commander. A second lieutenant, probably, not more than a few years older than Johnny.

"This machine's maximum range is only fifty yards, sir," said Johnny to the kid lieutenant.

"I know, I know. Two operators from our battalion already tried. They couldn't do it . . . and we lost 'em. Right before our eyes, we lost 'em."

Johnny knew what that meant. They'd fired their flame-throwers, missed their targets, and gotten themselves quickly killed by the Japs. *Next!*

"Ready?" said the lieutenant, now seemingly almost together. Whatever the explosive thing had done to put him in a daze, the effect was wearing off. Johnny'd seen some guys on the beach with dazes that would most likely never go away.

"Yes, sir," said Johnny to the lieutenant. He considered composing what might end up being a final Dear Betsy, but there wasn't time.

The officer said, "Raise your head up quickly and you can see our target. There's a slit about three feet wide, a foot tall. That's where they're shooting from."

Johnny did as ordered. He could see the concrete emplacement—just barely the slit.

"Put your fire into that hole and burn the bastards out of there," said the kid officer.

"Aye, aye, sir," said Private First Class Johnny Wrigley.

"It'll take some shooting . . . and some luck, I know. I'm sorry."

Sorry? Luck, my ass! I'm the best goddamn flamethrower operator in the whole goddamn marine corps! Watch this, Betsy! Sorry about the language.

Johnny brought the firing tool around into place and tried to figure how exactly to account for the longer distance, how he would have to adjust the height of the shot and thus the curve of the fire.

He grabbed the Zippo from his pocket. Now it was time for *him* to give orders.

"On a count of three, open the valves, sir. You say 'Ready' when you've done it. Then get out of the way."

Now Johnny was really excited. He was playing in a big game. He remembered the eighth-inning homer he'd hit with two on base against Westminster High in his junior year. That's how this felt. Nothing like what happened to football and basketball players, of course. They were the giants, the race-horses. Baseball was played by small and medium-size people who did gigantic things with small balls and opportunities. Johnny figured there were athletes of the body and the mind. Baseball players were the mind people. Muscle size helped, but that was it. It only helped.

Johnny closed his eyes, thought of the cheers that had come with that homer, took a deep breath.

"One . . . two . . . three."

He felt the movement with the napalm tanks. Johnny could only hope and pray that the kid lieutenant was enough out of his daze to do it right.

"Ready," the lieutenant said after what seemed way too much time to get those goddamn tanks open.

Johnny clicked the roller on the Zippo. It didn't ignite. He hit the lighter again. Nothing. And then a third time. Finally, it ignited. He lit the juice coming out of the nozzle.

And Johnny went to the firing position, adjusted the angle toward the bunker for what he believed would do the trick . . .

He squeezed the trigger.

With a whoosh, the stream of fire burst forward in its deadly arc.

After five seconds—a count of five in his head—Johnny let up on the trigger.

"You did it, Marine!" yelled the lieutenant. "Look at the little shits! Remember Pearl fucking Harbor! Remember Wake fucking Island. Remember the fucking Alamo!"

Johnny didn't pay attention to the lieutenant or look at anything. He took off running at a speed—even with the load on his back—that he felt was almost as fast as when he'd gone for that moving troop train in Kansas.

He heard several shots from small arms fire behind him as he ran, but none of them seemed aimed at him. At least, he didn't see—or, more important, feel—any coming his way.

He stopped and leapt into what appeared to be another crater—some kind of a hole that provided cover.

He looked up at the concrete bunker. Japs, their bodies on fire, were still running out. Marines, from positions Johnny couldn't make out, were picking the Japs off with rifle fire.

Let's hear it for some Miracle Whip—some cheers for Johnny Wrigley, our cleanup batter!

Then he heard the unmistakable terrifying pop and whistle of a mortar shell coming from the Japs' general direction. He looked back to where he had fired his beautifully aimed stream of liquid fire. The kid lieutenant was still there!

"Incoming, sir! Run! Run, sir!" Johnny yelled. But he knew it was too late. "You should have run, goddamn it, lieutenant . . ."

The mortar round landed, exploded, and, in what resembled a slow-motion sequence from the movie newsreels, blew the kid marine officer into many parts, up, up, and away.

It was the most horrible of the horrible sights Johnny Wrigley had seen.

So far.

ANDERSON'S DEATH HAD made him puke. Now that dazed kid officer's made Johnny just want to run far away as fast as he could.

He needed to be told it was not his fault that the lieutenant had died. That the kid-like-me had been a marine officer who should have known that he had to get out of there once the flamethrower was fired. But the lieutenant probably couldn't have done it because of whatever had happened to scramble up his brains before. It was probably a miracle—a Miracle

Whip for sure—that he had even been able to do what he'd done to help the flamethrower operation.

First Anderson. Now this guy. And already so many others on the landing craft and on the beach. His own time was probably coming. *Next!*

He began to work on something to say to Betsy. Not anything about dying or what was really going on. Maybe a story from his earlier life. But definitely not the Antietam tour. Maybe the story about the afternoon he'd spent in Baltimore going to the zoo. He'd been ten years old. A whole bunch of them had gone in on a school bus.

Johnny thought now about how the marines would send a marine in dress blues to the house in Lafayette to tell his mom that the Miracle Whip hadn't worked this time. Somebody official would have to tell her that her only child had died on an island nobody knows called Peleliu. She would cry and cry about her Johnny Oh, but she would feel better once the marine told her that her only son really had been one helluva flamethrower operator. That would be in addition to being one helluva baseball player who had had what it took to play center field for the Detroit Tigers someday.

Johnny wondered, but only for a few seconds, what some marine would say to that lieutenant's family when they brought the pieces of him back to them. *He died a hero, helping a PFC fry Japs, his brains so scrambled he couldn't remember to run.*

But Johnny's biggest worry was that nobody from the

marines would go to Kansas and tell his Betsy anything about Johnny Wrigley, the marine she'd met at the train station in Wichita, Kansas. He would hate her not knowing he was dead. But the official notification and burial unit in dress blues couldn't go see her because they didn't know her last name or where she lived. He hadn't even known where to send his letters, even if he had ever been able to write any. Any real ones.

There was still a lot of noise out there. . . .

But now, coming close, were footsteps, heavy breathing. *Goddamn it!* He had left his M1 back in that other hole with the dead lieutenant—what was left of him. Johnny tried to remember what he'd learned about hand-to-hand combat in a two-hour course he'd had at boot camp on how to kill people with his own two hands.

What came was another marine, throwing himself into the hole, almost on top of Johnny.

"What the hell!" the other guy grunted. The voice was familiar.

"Darwin! Is that you?"

"Jesus! Wrigley!"

They didn't embrace, though their legs were already intertwined just from where Darwin had landed.

"What are you doing over here?" Johnny asked. "I thought your regiment was way on the other side from us."

"Man, I don't know where my regiment is, where I am. We got hit bad right after we landed."

"Same with us. Everybody did."

"I see you're still a flamethrower man? Well, don't use that sonavabitchin' thing around me. I don't want to die with my balls on fire."

Johnny laughed. He couldn't help himself. It was crazy to laugh at such a thing. Both adjusted themselves as best they could to make room for the other. It was a tight fit.

"What are you going to do?" Johnny asked.

"Stay alive and find my outfit. Then stay alive some more until I can get off this goddamn awful place and go home to Mississippi and shoot birds instead of Japs."

"You shot any Japs?"

"Hell, no. All I've done is ducked and dodged while they shot at me."

"I got me some with this fire thing. Hit a real bull's-eye."

"Good for you. Like I say, just don't do it again till I'm out of here," Darwin said. And he still had something else on his mind.

"Wrigley, I want to know if you got laid in the couple of minutes we was in that Wichita place in Kansas. That's all I want to know before we die."

Johnny began to laugh but caught himself before it turned into a guffaw and then into something hysterical. "Yeah, I did," Johnny said without a second's thought. "Believe it or not, I really did."

"I knew it, Wrigley. I could see it in your eyes and in everything else. You got laid. You are not going to die a virgin like I am. Semper Fi, you lucky goddamn sonavabitching marine."

Darwin was groaning. Johnny couldn't tell if he was really upset or if he was faking it.

"What's the matter?" Johnny whispered. "God may have a plan for you that doesn't involve dying."

The words just came out. Johnny had never said anything like that before about God having a plan for his life. It all came from Betsy. *Yes!* Everything from here on out would come from Betsy.

"Tell me about it," said Darwin.

"What? About what?"

"Getting laid! Every detail. I'll close my eyes and imagine it's happening to me. What a way to die. Okay, Wrigley?"

Johnny had vowed, in private to her and to himself, never to tell anyone what had happened in that train station. But this was different. Stories between kid marines who thought they were about to die were different. That's what Johnny decided, at least.

Johnny sat up and, with Darwin's careful assistance, slid the flamethrower and knapsack off his back.

"Well, we just looked at each other there on that station platform. I took some Camels and an apple from her. She had the most beautiful brown eyes and sparkly face. Oh, my God, Darwin, she was gorgeous! Something just happened to both of us when we saw each other. I threw one of those apples way up there as far as I could . . ."

Johnny moved his right arm, replicating the throw even

though he knew Darwin wasn't watching. His eyes were already closed.

"The MPs were coming through looking for who'd done it—"

"I know about all that. Go to the screwing part," Darwin whispered. "I got to get on with it."

"Yeah, okay. She took me down into this little room where they stored all of the cigarettes and apples. There was a cot in there—"

"Good. Now we're cooking."

"I . . . well, I got all emotional about going to war, to combat, maybe dying. I lay down on the cot. She lay down next to me . . . you know, to comfort me, I guess you'd say. I didn't ask her to. She just did. She was that way—comforting. She did it for God. That's what she said. Something like that. She even prayed. Put her hands up together."

"Yeah, yeah."

"We clinched. You know, with our arms, and we were tight together. I touched her around herself and then kissed her. Maybe once or twice, maybe three times. Then one thing led to another . . . and that was it."

Johnny stopped. He wasn't sure he could say anything more.

"Lay it out, Wrigley. What exactly did you do—and she do?" Darwin was half sitting up now. His eyes were no longer closed.

Johnny glanced around. "There's not room enough to show you in here."

He moved reluctantly up to the rim of the crater and scooted out onto his stomach.

Then Johnny saw something in the air coming at him. It was a Jap grenade! With the automatic instinct of a star center fielder, he caught the goddamn thing with his bare right hand and, like going for the play at home plate, threw it hard in the direction it had come from.

He heard it explode off there somewhere.

Here's another one! No, there's *two* of them! Both in the air, one behind the other. He moved to his left, caught the first, and threw it back.

But he missed catching the other one. Number two landed in the hole with Darwin, who had dropped back down for cover.

There was a small explosion and then a huge burst of flame. The grenade had ignited what was left of the napalm in Johnny's flamethrower tanks.

"Aiiieeeeeeee!" Darwin screamed, his banshee sound penetrating Johnny's brain.

Keeping low, Johnny lunged toward the crater.

Darwin was on fire. He was no longer screaming. His hair, face, his everything was in flames. He was burning to a crisp— just like those Japs. And there was nothing Johnny could do to stop it.

Johnny fell to the ground and rolled himself over and over away from the fire—and Darwin.

It should have been Johnny in that hole. His mom's Oh Johnny Oh should have died. He didn't because of Betsy. He'd been talking about how he'd made love to her—even if it had been only for a few seconds.

He was away from Darwin, out of the crater, still alive because of her.

IT WAS JUST before five o'clock in the evening when he arrived in Wichita, Kansas, for the second time ever. This trip was on a real Santa Fe streamliner, still crowded and slow, but with passengers who were mostly civilians.

The war was over. Johnny Wrigley had survived. He was alive, ready to begin his new life with the girl he loved, the same girl whose brief presence at this same train station had kept him alive. She was his Betsy luck, his good luck charm for the war, for now, forever.

He was ready to have peace in his mind, a baseball in his throwing hand.

Johnny had been one of thousands of marines kept on Okinawa after the battle for the island had ended in June of 1945, until V-J Day in August. Another month went by before Johnny was put on a ship for the States. Then came months at a marine base called Camp Pendleton in California, south of Los Angeles.

Finally now, here he was in Wichita. He was shaking with alternating quivers of panic and excitement, not unlike how he'd felt going ashore with a flamethrower on his back. He'd hardly slept since he'd left California two nights and days ago.

Nearly two years had gone by since he'd left his Betsy at that train station. It was March and not as warm as it had been on that magic day in April.

"Magic" was definitely the word.

There—exactly *right* there—was where she had been standing when they'd first seen each other. When he'd come over to her, become enthralled by her bangs, had taken a pack of Camels. And then she'd said he had to have an apple, too. No apple, no cigarettes.

And he had grabbed an apple and thrown it as hard as he could like a baseball. Showing off his strong right arm.

Now, lugging his heavy dark green canvas duffle bag, he made his way through a swinging door marked STATION in foot-high black letters etched in glass. He kept moving down a concrete ramp. He remembered that ramp only vaguely as being about twenty feet wide, covered at the entrance by a gray stucco canopy with small glass windows. He also saw the sign that said TRACKS 2 AND 3.

And there, before a right turn toward the station waiting room, exactly where he remembered it to be, was a storeroom.

The storeroom.

He wanted—oh, God, how he wanted—one more miracle in his life. No more about mayonnaise. Just the fact of his being there meant that he had already had more than his share of real miracles, but he wanted to open the door and there she'd be, waiting for him. He'd take her in his arms, proclaim his survival of the war, say it really was because of her, profess his forever love.

The storeroom door was closed, just like it had been that April afternoon.

He set down his duffle, grabbed the brass doorknob, and opened the door.

"Station's on further around, Marine," said a man sitting behind a desk—the same desk that had been there before. The man was doing some paperwork, and he didn't stop doing it. He just gave Johnny a glance.

"Sorry. Thanks," said Johnny. "This was used for the women . . . the girls . . . who gave out cigarettes and apples to the troops on the trains."

"Yeah, right, that's what I hear," said the man, who Johnny figured was at least ten years older than he was and who was dressed in a dark blue railroad uniform—double-breasted coat with gold buttons and matching trousers. He was thin, drawn, starchy white. "I was away in Europe at the time myself. You in the Pacific?"

"That's right," Johnny said.

"I hear you guys had it worse and longer than we did."

The man now stood up. He clearly had work to do, but he seemed suddenly to decide that talking to this marine was more important.

"I'm Chapman," he said to Johnny, reaching out his right hand. "Where you headed?"

Johnny took the man's hand. "My name's Wrigley. I'm on my way home to Maryland."

"The Santa Fe gave me my job back with seniority—just like that. I'm a freight and baggage agent in charge of finding lost stuff. How about you?"

"I'm going to play ball. You know, with the pros."

"What position?"

"Center field."

"We have a lot of baseball around here in Wichita. The national semi-pro championship is played across the river at Lawrence Stadium."

Now Johnny saw the cot off in a corner. There was still a faint smell of apples and cigarettes, but the boxes of the Camels and the other smokes and the baskets were gone. So was the blackboard.

"I came through here on the way to the Pacific a while ago," said Johnny. "I'm looking for a girl I met that day."

Chapman shook his head and grinned. "Well, well, everything they say about you marines and girls must be true."

Johnny grinned back. "I want to look her up. I think I might have made her believe I'd probably die over there in the Pacific. I want her to know I didn't."

"Did she live here?"

"Yeah, sure—I think."

"Where exactly?"

"She didn't really say. I figured it had to be around Wichita—definitely in Kansas."

"What's her name?"

"Betsy."

"Betsy what?"

"Don't know . . . sorry to say."

Chapman sat down. But he didn't look at his paperwork. He kept engaged with Johnny. "I don't know what to tell you, Marine. There are probably a lot of Betsys in Kansas."

"There was a blackboard on a stand or something in here," said Johnny. "It had a lot of names on it. I think it was the duty list for the women—you know, the ones who met the trains that day. I saw some names. I don't remember any in particular. She said her name wasn't on it, but maybe it was."

Chapman got up and went to a cubbyhole over in a corner. He came back with the blackboard. "This it?"

"Yes, yes."

It was blank. Whatever had been written on it in the past had been erased, and the black slate had been given a thorough washing.

"Could there be paperwork around that would have names and dates?" Johnny asked.

The other man shook his head. "Sorry. There may have been some of that stuff, but it is long gone now. They either took it with them when the war was over or somebody came along and tossed it. Nothing was here when I got back."

"She—the girl—was kind of religious, I think. Does that help?" Johnny said.

"Everyone in Kansas is kind of religious," said the Santa Fe man with a laugh. "The state's still dry as a bone—can't buy a drink to save our lives or ruin our souls—except from the boot-leggers."

"She said she wanted to be a singer," Johnny added, knowing that there were probably a lot of girls in Kansas who wanted to be singers, too. Maybe even several million named Betsy?

A feeling of dumb-me frustration struck Johnny. What had ever made him think that after two years he could come back to Kansas and, with only a first name, find that girl? He had pleaded with the military transportation clerk in California to send him back to Maryland through Kansas with a train ticket that made it possible for him to stop over in Wichita for a while. Stupid, stupid, stupid. But what else could he do? Could he have done?

Dear Betsy,
   You are my future whole life.

That was about the last thing he had whispered before getting off the train.

Chapman was a man of sympathy. He took out a pocket watch and looked at it. "The stationmaster might remember something. He was here then because he was too old to go into the service. Follow me."

Johnny followed Chapman into the station, past the large array of ticket windows with ornate brass grates and stiff male agents behind them, to an office in the back.

The door was open, and they went in.

There sat a man dressed in a dark blue uniform similar to Chapman's. He wore a shiny black billed cap with a handsome silver badge on the front that said STATIONMASTER along with the name and emblem of the Santa Fe—a wide cross in a circle with the words "Santa Fe" in fancy type on the horizontal bar of the cross. The stationmaster, whose name Johnny did not get, was a big pleasant fellow who listened to Chapman quickly lay out what—*who*—Johnny was looking for. The older man—he was at least fifty, by Johnny's eye—remembered the basket women who'd met the troop trains. Certainly, he did. No records, though . . . except.

Johnny held his breath as the man dug through a file in a dark green metal cabinet and emerged with a single sheet of stationery paper. "The woman in charge was named Marsha Winston. Here's her address—and phone number. She lives here in Wichita. I'll bet she can help you."

Chapman and Johnny both thanked the stationmaster, who said, "Anything to help a marine. Chapman here, of course, is our own army hero. He was a P.O.W."

Johnny glanced at Chapman. His face had turned from his pale white to red.

"What's he talking about?" Johnny asked Chapman once they were outside in front of the huge station, which resembled a courthouse or big bank building. Chapman had insisted on escorting him on his way.

"I really don't want to talk about it," he said.

"Hey, I saw and did some things I'm never talking about either," Johnny said.

Chapman, his head down, said softly, "There's nothing to say."

"I'm sorry, sir," said Johnny.

"I was just a sergeant," said Chapman. "Don't 'sir' me."

"I'm just a corporal—and they made me that right before I was discharged."

Chapman looked up and smiled. Yes, he knew that two stripes on the sleeves meant corporal in the marine corps as it did in the army. "Where were you, Marine?"

Johnny waved the conversation to an end. He adjusted his duffle bag on his left shoulder. "It's almost dark. Maybe I'll wait till morning to see if I can find that troop train woman in charge. Any ideas on where I might get a room?"

Chapman pointed west. "This is Douglas Avenue, our main street. On the other side of the station, the tracks, and the underpass, there's a hotel called the Eaton. It's cheap, clean. It's even got some history to it. Good little café in there, too. I like to go by for coffee and a sandwich after work. Sometimes I visit with the bootleggers, too."

Johnny wasn't interested in bootleggers or any history of a

hotel. But that name, Eaton, sounded vaguely familiar to him. "Thanks, Soldier." Johnny had never in his life stayed in a hotel.

"Good luck, Marine," said Chapman. "You think you'd recognize that girl if you saw her again?"

Johnny tapped the side of his head with his right hand. "I see her every time I close my eyes. Sometimes even when they're wide open. I always see her."

That was not completely true. Sometimes on Peleliu he saw Anderson all smashed up, the smithereens of that dazed lieutenant, or Darwin burned to a blackened crisp.

And sometimes, the worst times, he saw the Okinawan kids and women he had, by mistake, incinerated with his goddamn flamethrower.

He had survived the hell of Peleliu so he could live through an even worse hell on Okinawa.

Johnny had so much never to tell anyone.

THE SECOND HE saw the sign for the Eaton Hotel, he realized why it was familiar. He had seen it out the troop train window nearly two years before.

Chapman had been right about the hotel being clean and cheap. For one dollar and seventy-five cents a night, he had a single bed, a private bathroom, a closet, and a small chest of drawers with a mirror on the wall over it. The bedspread was light blue and the towels and a washrag matched. There was another mirror over the sink in the bathroom. And there was a tiny bar of white soap in a paper wrapper with the Eaton's name on it. He had never had such a good place to stay as this, the first hotel room of his life.

But, even so, he knew he probably wouldn't sleep much that night.

He avoided looking in either of the mirrors.

Chapman, the poor guy, had had the look of a man who'd had experiences in Europe that he might never get over. *Same here, Santa Fe man.* Johnny wondered what it would take and how long it would take to get over Peleliu and Okinawa. Particularly Okinawa.

Johnny just couldn't wait until morning to get on with his search for Betsy.

So he dialed 4-5278, the number the stationmaster had given him for Marsha Winston, who lived on Ash Street in Wichita, Kansas. He identified himself and his mission.

"I cannot give out that kind of information about one of our girls, Corporal Wrigley," she said before he had even finished his spiel.

"I just want to tell her I didn't die," he said.

"If she had wanted to stay in touch in order that she would know such things, then she would have given you her address at the train station," said this Mrs. Winston.

Johnny tried to imagine what the woman must look like. Images of pointed-nosed witches and bitchy teachers flashed before him. The main teacher he had in mind was Miss DeShirley, who taught algebra. Definitely *not* Miss Lytton. She was a tall beautiful woman who, with the deep voice of a movie actress, entertained her students with captivating readings of famous poems and short stories. Johnny's liking of O. Henry came from Miss Lytton and her readings. She made a tradition of reading O. Henry's famous "The Gift of the Magi" at Christmastime.

Now Johnny so wished he had waited until morning to contact the troop train lady. Maybe she was a nicer person in the morning. That was the way his mom and other people often were.

Johnny was not going to surrender to this Mrs. Winston. Once more out of the amtrack and onto the beach!

"I fell in love with her," he said to the woman, who had talked to Johnny in a flat voice, not a thing like Miss Lytton's. "I want to marry her."

There was silence on the phone.

"I mean it, ma'am. I really do."

"That's not possible, Corporal," she said, but her tone was slightly changed—less hostile, more animated. "You couldn't have been with her more than a few minutes. Those troop trains stopped for only a half hour or so. People don't fall in love just like that."

"I did, ma'am."

"You have to get to know all about somebody before loving them," she said, her voice coming on as slightly more pleasant, more understanding. "You don't even know her name. How can you love her? Don't lie to me, Corporal Wrigley. Where are you from?"

"Maryland, ma'am."

"I should have known it was someplace like that. This is Kansas. We don't lie in Kansas."

They don't drink and they don't lie in Kansas. Isn't that just wonderful?

Johnny took several reinforcing deep breaths. He remained in landing assault mode. He said, "I know that's what it sounds like, but it's no lie. I mean it. Maybe I'm different from other guys. Maybe I can fall in love just like that, like being struck by lightning. Without knowing anything. I want to get down on my knees in front of her and ask her to spend the rest of her life with me. That's what I know. I also know that she brought me good luck. Having her in my memory kept me alive. Everybody else around me died, ma'am. But not me. She was my rabbit's foot."

There was another silence.

"When exactly did you say you came through here?"

Johnny wanted to shout with joy. *Made it to the beach!* He said, "April, two years ago."

"What day in April?"

"Toward the middle."

"What day of the week?"

"It was on a weekend, but the days were all running together at the time on that troop train. I think it was Sunday. Yes, I'm pretty sure it was Sunday. I got to California on April seventeenth, so whatever was the Sunday before that."

"Hold the line while I go see if I have anything that might help. I did keep some of our records. I thought someday our historical society might want them. Did you say you were a marine?"

"Yes, ma'am. And proud—"

He heard her put the phone down, so he didn't finish. Everyone in Kansas must know marines were proud of being marines anyhow.

More than a minute went by before she spoke again into the phone.

She said, "April fourteenth was a Sunday. We had twenty-two women at the station that day. We called them Trips of Joy. Most of the women on this day were from small towns around Wichita. They were in our organization named Sunflower Troop Train Women—S-T-T-W, which some of the ladies nicknamed 'Stews.' Short for both 'stewardesses' and good food, stew. They were of all ages. Only a few were very young girls along the lines you described."

Johnny heard the rustle of what sounded like papers. "I can't find a roster of names. It must be filed somewhere else, if one still exists."

"Would you mind looking some more?" Johnny asked.

"Not tonight, young man. I will see what I can find and get back to you tomorrow."

Johnny thanked her profusely and relayed his Eaton Hotel room number before saying a gentle good night and hanging up.

———

OH JOHNNY OH Wrigley had never had trouble crying when he was a boy. He had even done so when he was fifteen after he'd overthrown second base in a close game against Hancock, a throw that had cost a run and the game. More recently, just before he'd made love on that cot at the Wichita train station, he'd cried as well as shivered—almost. There had been tears in his eyes, at least.

Now he could not even tear up. Not since Peleliu. Or Okinawa. He had tried after Darwin had burned up, and after . . . and after and after and after. He couldn't even do it after what he'd done to those innocents on Okinawa.

After he put the receiver back on the phone in the hotel room, he tried again to cry. But he couldn't—not quite, not yet.

Instead, he left the room to get something to eat. He wasn't hungry. He just needed to do something. If he couldn't cry, maybe he could eat.

The elevator operator, a tiny old man in an oversize brown uniform with gold buttons, told him the food was fine in the coffee shop off the lobby.

"If you want something besides a bite, let me know," he said with a wink.

Johnny didn't get it.

The old man must have seen that in Johnny's face. "You can't buy a drink in this man's town, Soldier. Not even in Carry Nation's old bar. But I got a supply of Jack, as in Daniel's. That's what I'm saying."

"Marine. I'm a marine, not a soldier."

"Okay, fine. You know about that old biddy Carry Nation?"

When Johnny didn't respond, the elevator man said, "She's the main reason you can't get a drink in Kansas. She even came into this hotel back in 1900 and chopped up the bar, wrecked a fancy mirror in the name of God and demon whiskey. She was a religious nut. They're everywhere around here."

Johnny decided the bar chopping and mirror smashing was the history thing the Santa Fe man had been talking about. He also concluded this was the slowest elevator in the world. His room was only on the fifth floor, but it seemed like they'd already been in transit for a week or so.

The man in charge of the trip patted his breast in a spot where he must have had a pint of whiskey. "If you have a need for Jack as in Daniel's, I'm right here. My prices are as cheap as you'll find this side of Atchison, Topeka, *or* Santa Fe."

Johnny didn't want anything to drink. He had had the sum total of two beers and a glass of whiskey in his life, and none had gone down well. The taste was awful, like turpentine. But it was more than that. Johnny had always been concerned about what drinking might do to his reflexes and concentration, what it could do to his keeping both eyes on a breaking ball or a really high fly ball.

The Eaton was a bus station as well as a hotel, something Johnny hadn't really noticed when he'd checked in. The lobby was divided roughly into two sections, with the front desk on one side, and another counter, which he now saw was for bus tickets, on the other. There were several fairly nice overstuffed chairs and couches scattered around on a white tiled floor, along with small tables of magazines and newspapers for hotel guests and bus passengers. Only a few chairs were occupied now.

The coffee shop was small, with maybe eight tables, four booths, and a string of stools at a counter. There were only a half dozen customers, all of them men. One put his hand to his forehead in a salute when Johnny came in.

"Good job, Soldier."

Johnny decided not to correct this guy. What difference did it make anymore anyhow? He was technically no longer a marine. His discharge had been effective the day they'd given him his final papers and the transportation clerk had sent him on his way back to his place of enlistment. He was already a civilian. But what mattered to Johnny was that he still considered himself a marine until he quit wearing his uniform. And since he had no civilian clothes, that would not happen until he either bought some or got home.

He went to a booth in a corner and ordered a Velveeta cheese sandwich on white bread with chips and a Coke. The menu was cardboard, printed on both sides. After giving his order to a friendly middle-aged waitress, he turned over the menu.

There was the Carry Nation story, just as the guy on the elevator had told it.

This is some strange place, Kansas, he thought.

What if Betsy insisted on staying here, living here? How would they have a life with her in Kansas and him running around wherever, playing baseball? Johnny had read in the paper that wives don't get to travel with the players—not even in the majors.

He decided against doing any new Dear Betsys right now. Not yet. Maybe not until he found her—forever and for life.

After he had eaten, Johnny took a slow walk around the lobby before heading back upstairs. There were copies of two Wichita newspapers on the tables. The headlines were about plans for war crimes trials against Nazis in Germany and about MacArthur running things in Japan. He opened one of the papers, *The Wichita Eagle,* to the sports page. The semi-pro teams were losing their pros. There was much being written about the return of the veterans—Joe DiMaggio and Hank Greenberg from the army, Ted Williams from flying planes for the marines, and, of course, Pistol Pete, back from having played ball for the army at Fort Riley, up the road somewhere in Kansas. Spring training was about to begin for the majors and the minors. That was where Johnny wanted to be, soon and forever.

Johnny moved on to the bus ticket counter. There was a blue and yellow poster board that proclaimed that Kansas Central Lines buses left from there. The company was called "The Route of the Flint Hills," whatever they were.

And underneath that it listed four round-trips a day from

Wichita to Abilene, with intermediate stops in Sedgwick, Newton, North Newton, Goessel, Hillsdale, Marion, Elmo, and Lehighton.

JOHNNY HUNG UP his uniform in the closet. His tan cotton shirt was wrinkled from sitting up on the train from California, but his dark green woolen tunic was okay, and the trousers still had a crease. He had another clean shirt he could put on in the morning.

Or maybe he would buy some civvies. But Betsy might not recognize him out of uniform. Maybe he would wait until he found her before switching to civilian clothes.

He lay down on the bed in his white T-shirt and boxer shorts. That was standard marine underwear. Most everything about him remained standard marine. But not for much longer.

He must have slept a few minutes here and there during the night, but he didn't really know for sure. He remembered getting up and going to the head—the bathroom—a few times, careful to keep the light out so he wouldn't see himself in the mirror.

As always, he mostly remembered lying in bed with his eyes open after losing sight of Betsy's face for a while.

The burning bodies and the screams of those kids on Okinawa came back.

As always.

The Jap soldiers had taken them into that cave with them. But Johnny hadn't known that. The sound from their screaming went through Johnny's ears, down inside him somewhere, and wouldn't come out and go away.

Like Chapman, the Santa Fe man, he wondered if it ever would.

He had decided that he would never tell anybody about those kids. That included his Betsy—even after they were married. He would tell her about Darwin, of course, because it was talking about what they had done in the train station storeroom that had saved his life. But he wouldn't go into a lot of detail. He'd just say a grenade had killed the other man in the hole. And he wouldn't tell her, of course, exactly what he'd told Darwin about what they'd done. He would say just that he had been going on and on about how he had fallen in love at first sight with this beautiful Kansas girl at the Wichita train station.

Playing ball again would probably help. It's hard to see and hear burning kids while deciding in a split second whether to take or swing on a 3-2 count or dive for a falling fly ball in short center.

So he hoped.

And now, in the morning daylight, he waited a couple of hours for the phone to ring, for Mrs. Winston of the Stews to call with more information on Betsy. He was going to need Betsy *and* baseball.

There was no call. So, after alerting the front desk about the possibility of his receiving an urgent message from "a Mrs. Winston," Johnny went out on the streets of Wichita. He thought it might be possible simply to come across his Betsy. Bump into her at an intersection. See her sitting at a café sipping a cup of coffee, walking down the street, waiting on somebody in a store. She had to live around there somewhere. Why wouldn't she come to downtown Wichita on a Tuesday morning? Miracles really *do* happen, he already knew that.

He was in full uniform, feeling fairly squared away in a fresh shirt. He had once again shaved and tied his tan uniform tie and put on his tunic blouse and cap without looking at himself. His cap was one of those simple folded ones that slipped over the top of the head like a small half a sack. They were officially known as overseas caps. Marines called them piss cutters.

Johnny didn't need light or mirrors to square himself away. He had learned in the marines how to do most everything in the dark, including assembling the many parts of a flamethrower.

The last time he had taken a good look at his face was aboard the ship coming home. He didn't like the red rims around his eyes. He particularly didn't like the person he saw. He didn't want to look at a man who had murdered kids, even if he hadn't meant to.

Johnny hoped Betsy wouldn't notice too much change in him from two years before.

The last thing he did before leaving the hotel room was brush his teeth long and hard. Even though he had kept his vow to Betsy not to chew tobacco again, he wanted to make double sure his mouth tasted okay for her now.

"Hey, Marine!"

It was a man's voice behind him.

Johnny turned to see another marine. This one was older, in dress blues. At a glance Johnny saw that he was a gunnery sergeant—three red and yellow peaked stripes over two half circles on both sleeves of his dark blue tunic.

"You lost, Corporal?" said the sergeant.

"Naw, just walking around, Gunny," Johnny replied. "Gunny" was what marines called gunnery sergeants, second only to master sergeant as the top enlisted rank in the Corps. "I'm kind of between trains."

The sergeant said his name was Holcomb and he was in charge of the marine recruiting station across the street in the post office building. He was at least fifteen years older than Johnny, and thirty pounds heavier. A real marine.

The two shook hands. There was no saluting. That was for officers. Johnny noticed the ribbons on the other man's chest. There was a Bronze Star with a combat V and a Purple Heart. "Where'd you get those, Gunny?"

"Tarawa," said the gunny. "War's over now, though, which means no recruits to hustle anymore. Easy duty."

That duty, Johnny figured, probably also once had included attending funerals and informing moms and others of bad news about some marines.

"Where *you* been?" the gunny asked Johnny after an obvious glance at the four ribbons over the left chest pocket of his uniform blouse. They were only for having participated in specific battles in the Pacific. Nothing personal.

"Peleliu and then Okinawa." Johnny just said it. He had thought he might never do that. But this guy was also a marine. This was different.

"Peleliu? My God, Corporal." Gunnery Sergeant Holcomb stiffened, took a step back, and snapped off a perfect marine-to-officer salute. "I honor your service."

"Thank you," Johnny mumbled. He had heard before leaving California that the word about the horror and the heavy casualties of Peleliu had spread throughout the marine corps—particularly among the career professionals. A staff sergeant from his battalion had told the story about everyone in a noncommissioned officers club in San Diego standing up, yelling "He was at Peleliu!" and raising a glass to him. This was Johnny's first experience with such a thing.

"What can I do for you?" said Gunny Holcomb. "Name it. You want a meal, a drink, a ten-dollar bill—a girl?"

"Not a thing, really," said Johnny quickly. "I'm just getting some exercise before hopping onto another train."

"Semper Fi, then," said Holcomb. That was the short version of the marine motto of Semper Fidelis—always faithful. It was a kind of password between marines.

"Semper Fi, Gunny."

A girl. Johnny wanted to tell Gunny Holcomb about *the* girl, about meeting her here in Wichita two years before, about the life-important need to find her now so he could ask her to marry him.

But that would not be very marine, asking a man who had

won the Bronze Star and Purple Heart on Tarawa to do such a personal, unmilitary thing.

He was sure there was nothing the gunny could do to help find her anyhow.

Johnny returned to the Eaton. A room clerk told him there were no messages.

SO HE KEPT walking.

Chapman, the Santa Fe army man, had told him Douglas was the main street through Wichita from Union Station west several blocks to a river. Wichita had the look and feel of a bigger place than the one he'd seen from train windows. No, it wasn't Baltimore, but it was certainly in that class. A real city.

In the ten or so downtown blocks there were shoe stores; restaurants; at least three department stores, including a big one called Buck's; a couple of radio stations; some dime stores; three banks; and lots and lots of Kansas people.

His Betsy wasn't one of them.

He knew she wouldn't be in one of the four movie theaters sprinkled around downtown Wichita. She had said she didn't believe in movies. Too bad, because one of the Wichita theaters, called the Orpheum, was showing *Abilene Town,* starring the one and only Randolph Scott! Johnny loved the coincidence of there now being Mr. Scott in a new movie about Abilene, Kansas. The big posters outside had a half-dressed saloon girl played by Rhonda Fleming, and off to the side the smiling tough-guy face of Mr. Scott. "Ablaze with

Guns and Guts and Glory" was printed below "Abilene Town" in larger type.

There was another poster near a door of the Orpheum. It urged "girls of Kansas" to enter the Miss Kansas bathing beauty and talent pageant at the theater in July. The winner would receive an all-expenses-paid trip to Atlantic City to compete for Miss America and win $25,000 in scholarship prizes.

Johnny knew Betsy would make a great Miss Kansas *and* Miss America. But he was sure she would never enter such a contest because it was probably against her religion—like everything else. That was good, in this case. Johnny wouldn't want Betsy walking around in public in a swimsuit.

When he got to the river, he saw a baseball stadium off to the left on the other side of the bridge. He figured that had to be the semi-pro place Chapman had been talking about.

Johnny kept moving over the bridge toward the stadium. Why not give it a look?

There were a few dusty cars and pickups in the parking lot, and he heard baseball sounds from inside—bats against balls, balls into mitts, chatter. Some kind of practice must have been under way.

LAWRENCE STADIUM, said a big sign over the front entrance. Beneath it in even larger letters was: HOME OF THE NATIONAL BASEBALL CONGRESS CHAMPIONSHIP.

He walked through an open gate into the empty concessions and ticket area. This was a real baseball stadium—twice the size of the field at Shepstown and the other minor league fields he'd seen before the war. There were concrete stands behind home plate and the dugouts, as well as wooden bleachers down the foul lines. Good solid white lines on the diamond, good grass. The concrete outfield wall had a dark green section in dead center like in the pros' stadiums. That was to provide a good background for batters to better see the white ball coming at them from the pitcher's mound.

A team was practicing—hitting, base running, making double plays. Some pitchers and catchers were also throwing. He saw COLEMAN LANTERNS across the front of their uniforms. Clearly a semi-pro team.

There was nobody in the stands but Johnny. He sat down and watched. This was his world, the one away from Peleliu and Okinawa, his memories—and even Betsy. Baseball, semi-pro or pro—this was where he belonged.

He thought about going out on the field and asking if one of the players would let him just hold a ball for a while—for a minute or even just a few seconds.

But he decided not to. And after a few minutes, he went back across the bridge to downtown, to Broadway, which seemed to him to be the major north-south cross street. There was another department store, two more big hotels, which, like the Broadview, were much fancier than the Eaton. There was also a huge Trailways bus depot, which was full of yellow and red buses with the names of big cities in their destination signs—Chicago, Dallas, Tulsa, Los Angeles, Denver, Omaha.

That small company at the Eaton seemed to have had buses going only to towns in Kansas.

Betsy wasn't in the big bus depot, in the stores, or in the other places or on the sidewalks along Broadway either.

He moved up and down other cross and parallel streets along Broadway and north and south of Douglas. There were newspaper offices, a store with cast-iron fire trucks and other great toys in the window, a Masonic temple, and a tiny ten-cent-a-hamburger joint called a Kings-X, where he eventually had lunch. They didn't have any kind of cheese sandwiches so he ordered a burger and a Coke. He drank the Coke and ate the burger, which was so small it was gone in two bites.

And soon he was back outside walking again. If Betsy was out there, maybe on a stroll down Douglas or up Broadway, he didn't want to miss her. The tiny burger was fine anyhow. He hadn't been hungry, hadn't been really since that pre-invasion breakfast before Peleliu. He mostly ate because he had to, not because he wanted to.

Betsy would change that. Yes, she would. The two of them would sit down together, put away good meals of meatloaf and mashed potatoes, sausage patties and home fries, chocolate cake and apple pie. You bet, apple pie. He just knew that she was a great cook. She was great at everything she did. He could just tell that.

Then, almost as if a Jap sniper had put a bullet into his head, he knew it was over. Crack! Splat! The end! He wasn't going to find her. Betsy from Kansas had been in his life for only a few minutes, and that was that. There might still be an occasional Dear Betsy. Maybe there might always be Dear Betsys. But no real Betsy.

He didn't have a wristwatch, but he saw from a big clock over a bank that it was after three o'clock in the afternoon. He had been walking since ten that morning. There was not a face of a young woman or girl anywhere along his way that he hadn't looked at carefully, matching it always with the snapshot he carried with him in his mind.

She wasn't there.

Betsy isn't here.

He made his way to Buck's, the big department store, and bought himself a set of civvies—a cream-colored long-sleeved sport shirt and brown slacks that were pleated. He decided to wear them out of the store, carefully placing his marine uniform in a Buck's sack.

The marines was over.

He went back to the train station. With the help of Chapman, the ex-army Santa Fe man, he got a reservation on the next day's first train east. Santa Fe had an eight o'clock morning departure on the Chicagoan to Kansas City and Chicago, with connections to Baltimore.

Johnny Oh had to go on to baseball.

Then he went back to the Eaton.

There was a message from Mrs. Winston, which Johnny immediately returned.

"I did find a roster for that Sunday, Corporal," she said.

Johnny closed his eyes as he held the phone receiver to his ear, held his breath—his life.

"There were no Betsys on it, I am sorry to say. We had two Susans, a Susie, a couple of Joans and Jeannes—a Beth, a Janet, even a Lena. But not a single Betsy."

"What about her going by a middle name?" he asked.

"The lists included both first and middle names. No Betsy."

Johnny had nothing else to say.

Mrs. Winston said: "There is only one small item that could be helpful. Of the twenty-two girls on duty that April Sunday, the youngest were from one or two different towns. Some were no more than seventeen or eighteen years old. Most of the others were older, but these younger girls were doing their first Trip of Joy, if I recall correctly. It's hard to remember precisely, of course, because we had so many go through our station during the war."

Johnny didn't get it. "But if she was Betsy, then why wasn't she on the list as Betsy?"

Mrs. Winston, now speaking almost sweetly in the tone of a loving aunt, said, "A possible explanation is that we often suggested that our Stews not give their real names to the troop train soldiers. It sometimes made it easier for the girls to remain . . . you know, less vulnerable to the development of uncomfortable or unwanted relationships. I recall saying that most particularly to the youngest and least experienced . . . if you understand?"

Johnny understood all right. "So one of the young ones could be my Betsy?"

"It's possible. That is all I can say."

"Where do they live?"

"That's the problem. There's nothing in our records that gives the specific hometowns of the twenty-two. But it was possibly Hillsdale or, most likely, Lehighton."

"Lehighton? Where is that?"

"Now, Corporal, let me emphasize that I do not know for sure Lehighton was the town. It could just as well have been Hillsdale. But they do sing the Messiah in Lehighton. You said something about the girl being a singer."

"Where is Lehighton, ma'am?"

"It's just over an hour north on the Kansas Central bus—"

Johnny thanked her and raced as fast as he could down to the bus ticket counter in the Eaton lobby.

AND, AS LUCK would have it, there was a bus to Lehighton just a few minutes later. Was that a simple coincidence, or did this mean another real Miracle Whip was on its way for Johnny Wrigley? His Betsy luck was holding?

Whatever was to be eventually, there sat a happy Johnny in the first row on the tiny Kansas Central Lines bus, which, counting Johnny, had only six passengers in its nineteen seats. Although the bus was painted in bright blue and yellow colors, the windows rattled and it had a horrific motor whine and a huge exhaust cough that made Johnny think it was hovering near the bus version of death. The driver apologized for the bus, which he called a Clipper. He said its hard wartime service had left it with a wide array of defects, including a habitual overheating problem that required frequent stops to put water in the radiator.

"What are the girls like in Lehighton?" Johnny asked the driver after a while.

"They're mostly just like any of our own Kansas girls," said the driver. "They're mostly pretty and good—good and religious."

The driver was a skinny man, clearly, like the stationmaster, too old to have been in the service. He was dressed in a well-worn uniform of a frayed gray dress shirt, black pants, and tie. The bus tires were kicking up clouds of dust on the gravel until they hit pavement only the last twenty-five miles before Lehighton.

"Do they happen to sing a lot, too?" Johnny asked the driver. "I'm looking for a pretty girl who is religious and sings."

The driver gave Johnny a quick hard glance. The new civvies made it obvious that here was a kid just out of the service. He was okay. Give him a break, even if he's going after our Kansas girls. So he said, "Some sing, some don't. Most everybody does at the 'Messiah' in Lehighton, though. Probably even some who shouldn't."

Johnny didn't follow exactly what the man was saying, but he was encouraged. When you're in mind for a miracle, everything's encouraging.

Out the bus window, he saw fields of wheat, sorghum, and hay. And there were those big grain elevators and small towns Johnny remembered from the earlier train trip, and a lot of dirt and gravel roads, railroad crossings, small farmhouses, tractors, pickup trucks, wire fences, old horses, thin cows, fat pigs.

This was Kansas—central Kansas. Was this his Betsy's place? Maybe Wichita and troop trains of marines were not.

He so hoped she'd agree to come with him to Maryland and, eventually, to Detroit.

And there came blacktop pavement and the outskirts of his destination—maybe even his destiny.

There was a multicolored wooden sign that featured life-size painted portraits of a man and a woman. Each was in a light blue choir robe, holding a hymnal, and looking to the heavens. Below them in bold black letters was:

> Welcome to Lehighton, Kansas
> Home of Calvary College
> and
> The "Messiah" Capital of the World
> Population 5,300

"That 'capital' stuff may be a bit of a stretch, because there are other places in the U.S. and the world that have larger annual Easter or Christmas singings of the thing," said the driver.

His bus chugged through downtown toward the Skelly Oil gas station, where a small metal blue and yellow ticket office sign in the shape of a sunflower hung from the front.

Johnny got off the bus and then stayed with the driver while he refilled the radiator, for what the driver could tell him about the " 'Messiah' thing." Finally Johnny got it. The "Messiah" was at least two hours of chorus singing about the Crucifixion and Resurrection of Jesus Christ. Johnny had heard the whole

Bible story a couple of times at school, of course, but not a long musical version of it.

"The girls sing the 'Messiah' thing?" he asked the driver.

"Most everybody in town sings—boys and girls, grown men and women, hundreds of them on a stage with a student orchestra and soloists," answered the bus man. "It's even on the radio in Kansas City sometimes. They're doing rehearsals now for the big early spring, and then Easter stuff over at the college auditorium only a few blocks away."

Johnny was on his way as fast as he could run in the direction of another Miracle Whip.

"DES-PIS-ED . . . HE WAS des-pis-ed . . . re-ject-ed, he was des-pis-ed and re-ject-ed of men; a man of sor-rows, and ac-quaint-ed with grief, a man of sor-rows, and ac-quaint-ed with grief . . ."

Those were the words Johnny heard the moment he entered the auditorium. He was still barely inside the enormous place. Calvary College's Messiah Hall, which smelled of varnish and hymnbooks, seemed as long and as tall as a circus tent. Johnny figured you could play baseball in there, it was so big.

There was only a scattering of twenty or thirty people sitting downstairs or in the balcony among what looked like two or three thousand fold-up wooden seats. Johnny moved on down one of the side aisles.

A young woman, standing on a stage with a couple of other soloists in front of the huge chorus, was the one singing about the des-pis-ed and re-ject-ed. She was alternating with more voices from a chorus, male and female, of several hundred people. Most everyone was in casual dress. This was definitely a rehearsal, as the bus man had said.

Johnny was about halfway down the far right aisle toward the stage, watching now more than he was listening.

The young woman soloist had a look to her . . . something familiar.

Betsy? Are you Betsy?

He moved almost to the edge of the seating area and looked up at the singer. Nobody, including the woman, seemed to pay any attention.

Johnny could see that her hair was not exactly like his Betsy's. The bangs had disappeared. The reddish blondness was gone. Her hair, now more of a regular brown color like that on a man's dress shoes, was swept up from the middle of her head to each side. And it was shorter. The brown eyes seemed a bit lighter. And greenish. Her dress, sky-blue with a white collar and short sleeves, showed off her body. She was some-what thinner than Betsy—as he remembered her from those few minutes. Her shoes were white canvas like tennis shoes. Johnny couldn't imagine Betsy wearing such things. But the voice. It sounded a lot like her. And she *was* a singer. She also had a lot more lipstick and rouge on her face than he remembered from the train station. People change, of course. And it had been two years. . . .

Johnny eased back a few steps as the soloist stopped singing.

A man in the front of the stage yelled out: "Let's go through the big one another time before we take a break! Okay?"

Everybody leapt to their feet. There was a huge burst of sound from the orchestra and the full chorus, unlike Johnny had ever experienced.

The male singers shouted:

> *"King of kings!"*

And the girls sang:

> *"For-ev-er and ev-er*
> *Hal-le-lu-jah*
> *Hal-le-lu-jah*
> *For-ev-er and ev-er*
> *Hal-le-lu-jah*
> *Hal-le-lu-jah."*

Again, the men yelled:

> *"And Lord of Lords!*
> *For-ev-er and ev-er*
> *Hal-le-lu-jah*
> *Hal-le-lu-jah . . ."*

The women joined in, some of them singing in high-pitched soprano voices, others lower. And everybody, the men and the women, went on and on, back and forth, mostly with hallelujahs. Johnny had never heard anything like it. The sounds seemed to fill the air and space all the way to the wavering ceiling and the shaking walls of the gigantic hall.

For a moment Johnny thought he might actually cry—finally. *What the hell is this?* No music had ever done that to him before. A war and dead marines and Okinawan kids hadn't done it either.

Then with several concluding thunderous hallelujahs, it ended. Snap, like somebody had turned a switch. Just like that, the music was over. The audience, including Johnny, were now permitted to breathe. Johnny's crying urge was over, too.

"Take thirty!" ordered the man on the stage. He was dressed in old khaki pants and a gray sweatshirt, he was at least forty years old, and he had the deep voice and presence of a marine drill instructor. Johnny had a feeling that the guy had definitely been in the war. Maybe not a marine but something in the service. He was back, a civilian, now helping people sing about the story of Jesus again. Just like Johnny and Pete Reiser, civilians, would now play center field again.

Johnny kept his eyes on the soloist, the one who resembled Betsy. She left the stage with a couple of other female singers and walked out a side door of the auditorium.

Johnny followed from maybe twenty yards away. There

were movements in her hips that he thought he recognized. They seemed a lot like Betsy's. Wasn't there something, too, about the way she flung her shoulders back?

And yet, she just didn't seem to really fit. She wasn't that magnificent star of a beautiful girl he loved—so deeply, so immediately, so forever.

And yet . . .

He followed her and the others across a narrow sidewalk through a lawn of perfectly mowed bright green grass, shrubs, and red and yellow flowers. They went up a few steps into a redbrick building with GEORGE FRIDERIC HANDEL HALL embedded in concrete over the door.

Inside was a large room full of shelves of books and magazines, racks of choir robes, many music stands, a bass violin, a tuba, a baby grand, and an upright piano. Most of the wall space was covered with various-size framed drawings and paintings of one man in particular. Johnny assumed it had to be George Frideric Handel.

The girl moved over to a corner sitting area, which consisted of two dark red corduroy overstuffed chairs and a small table. She sat down in one of the chairs by herself and held a thick book of music.

Johnny went over to her. "Hello there," he said. "I am looking for Betsy."

The soloist looked up at him with a smile that was almost exactly as pleasant and unique and divine as the one he'd seen on Betsy's face two years ago—*almost* exactly. "There are no

Betsys here," she said in a way of speaking that sounded more precise—more like a solo singer—than Betsy would have. "At least not in the 'Messiah.'"

Johnny moved slightly closer. He wanted to make absolutely sure she could see his face as well as he could see hers. Maybe his freckles even? "I thought maybe she might be a singer in the 'Messiah' thing?"

The soloist-who-could-be-Betsy just shook her head. "I know everyone here. This is our music department building. I know that nobody named Betsy is in the chorus or the orchestra."

"You're one of the main singers, is that right?" he asked.

"Yes. There are four of us. This is my first time to sing one of the solo parts. I've always been in the chorus—since junior high school, as a matter of fact. I'm nervous about it all."

"Don't be," said Johnny Oh.

"Well, I need to go through my parts a bit more now before we resume rehearsal. . . ."

"May I ask what your name is?"

"Donna Jo. Donna Jo Hesston."

They looked at each other directly as they spoke.

Donna Jo Hesston clearly did not recognize the young freckle-faced man in the brown pleated slacks and cream-colored shirt.

Donna Jo Hesston was not Betsy. Not *his* Betsy, at least.

"Did you ever go to the Wichita train station to give away cigarettes and apples at the troop trains?" he asked finally. Just to make 100 percent sure.

"Certainly not," she said, rather too indignantly, it seemed to Johnny. What was wrong with being nice to a bunch of marines taking a break off a troop train?

"Did you know of anybody—any girls—who did?"

"There were a few from here and some of the other towns around," she said. "But I didn't know many personally."

"Were any of them singers?" Johnny asked. It would be his next-to-last question—almost.

"None that I knew of," Donna Jo Hesston replied, now sounding a bit testy.

"You ever sing 'Haunted Heart'?"

"No, no. We don't do a lot of popular music here at Calvary College," said Donna Jo Hesston. "Now I really do need to get to work on the 'Messiah.'"

"What brand of religion are you?" he asked, intentionally making it sound like a question he'd ask a clerk at his mom's grocery store.

"Lutheran," was the girl's answer. "We all are."

Johnny couldn't resist. "How do you Lutherans like Miracle Whip?" he asked Donna Jo Hesston.

Frowning and shaking her head, she replied, "We prefer the real mayonnaise."

JOHNNY JUMPED OFF the bus at Wichita and immediately found the Eaton's bootlegging elevator operator. He bought a pint of Jack as in Daniel's bourbon whiskey for two dollars and fifty cents.

Then he took the pint into the café that used to be a bar and poured a third of it into a heavy white china coffee cup.

He sat at a far end of the counter, where he could not see his own face in the large mirror that the historical plaque said was a replica of the one the anti-liquor lady had smashed along with the bar.

"Not really legal, you know, to drink like that in our place," said the man behind the counter of the café. "But you were in the war, so maybe we'll give you some special rights."

Johnny emptied the cup in four steady, uninterrupted swallows.

The stuff went down so fast Johnny barely noticed the whiskey taste, which, to him, vaguely resembled the smell of gasoline—or maybe napalm from a flamethrower.

"Easy there, son," said a customer at the café counter. "Were you army?"

"Marine. I was a U.S. marine." Johnny filled the cup again. And he downed it all again.

"Hey, kid, be careful now. At least put some water in it. Or some soda and ice."

Johnny didn't even glance over toward him or the two other customers. Johnny had no idea what they actually looked like, fat or skinny, old or young.

"How old are you, anyhow?" one of the customers said to Johnny.

"Twenty. Almost twenty years old."

"That's not old enough, son."

"For what?"

"Drinking whiskey—even illegally."

"What about for burning people to a crisp? Am I old enough to do that?"

The whiskey bottle was almost empty.

"What about not finding my Betsy? Am I old enough for that?"

The bottle was now completely empty.

Johnny, without even moving his head, remained absolutely still and silent for at least two minutes. So did everyone else in the café. Then Johnny yelled out in the direction of the lobby and the elevator man. "Need a refill!"

None of the four men in the café said anything.

Several minutes went by. No whiskey was delivered.

Johnny grabbed a large glass sugar dispenser from the counter in front of him. He held it tight in his right fist, flung his arm behind him, and threw the thing hard at a glass case of pies behind the counter.

There was a loud crash, and most of the pies were a mess. "Need a refill!" Johnny shouted again.

Finally the old elevator man rushed into the café with another bottle of Jack Daniel's. Johnny gave him three one-dollar bills and told him to keep the change.

"Look here now, Marine," said the café man. "You can't bust up my business like this. I don't want to involve any cops, but I will if I have to."

Johnny tossed some money onto the counter without counting it.

The white cup was filled another time. So was Johnny's mouth and throat with Jack as in Daniel's.

Johnny now saw more than four faces in the café. Suddenly he was dizzy, sick.

His forehead fell down hard onto the counter in front of him.

"Hey, Marine, is that you?" Somebody was yelling something at him.

Johnny raised his head slightly and managed a weak smile.

"It's me, Chapman. The Santa Fe man. I came by for a sandwich. . . ."

Johnny raised the white cup in his right hand and, as if it were his final act, threw it at an angle at the mirror. It had the velocity of a weak lob, and it didn't even come close.

Then Johnny closed his eyes and slipped off the counter stool as if he'd made a wrong step on a landing craft net. He fell into the arms of Chapman, who held him tightly for dear life.

JOHNNY SPENT MOST of the night inside his bathroom's toilet bowl, his head banging with pain, his mouth full of the taste of vomit. Never had he been so miserable, so ill, so desperate to end it all—all of what that demon whiskey Jack Daniel's and his own childish idiocy had done to him.

Chapman, with the help of a porter, put Johnny on board the Chicagoan at eight o'clock the next morning for the trip to Kansas City, Chicago, and points east—home to Maryland.

There was no color in Johnny's face; even his freckles seemed to have disappeared along with most of his insides.

"There's no hangover so bad it won't go away in about twenty-four hours," Chapman said. "You'll be in Chicago by then." Those were this good Kansas ex-soldier's farewell words to the Maryland ex-marine living through his first drunk.

Johnny's agony did not permit the speaking of words in a conversation, even important last ones to Chapman. "Thanks. I really thank you." That was all Johnny could manage. His voice was a whispered peep of a little boy's.

The sounds and the jars of the train added to Johnny's misery. He wondered if it was possible to barf so ferociously that eventually a drunk man's stomach itself, including such parts of the anatomy as the belly button, would come rising up through the mouth?

Johnny had no idea how long he sat there, his head leaning half on the headrest of the seat, half on the train window. His eyes were closed but only to prevent seeing and thus experiencing motion that would have added even more dizziness to his state of being. He remembered a conductor calling out the names of towns before the agonizing lurches that preceded station stops. He thought he heard the names "Newton!" and "Emporia!" And, after a long while, he knew for a fact that this huge station was in Kansas City.

That was just after twelve noon. He wasn't exactly sure how he knew that, but maybe there'd been a big clock on a passing building, like on the banks in Wichita.

Johnny actually stood up from his seat on the train for the first time and walked around outside on the station platform.

Some fresh air was breathed. Real steps by real feet were taken. He bought a Coke from a train-side vendor, a distinguished-looking black man in a perfectly laundered and pressed white service coat and perfectly pressed black trousers. The nausea was diminishing. There were signs of life once again in Johnny Wrigley.

And, for the rest of the day, Johnny continued his recovery as he traveled through Missouri, remembering it from that first trip as something called the Show-Me State—whatever in the hell that meant. Show me what? How to get drunk on Jack Daniel's? To play center field? He was able to read the signs at train stations—Marceline and La Plata were two of them. He ate a cheese sandwich without repercussions. Cheese sandwiches, cold on white bread with mayonnaise, or grilled, had always been his favorite thing to eat. His mom, whatever else was going on, had always had on hand plenty of everything it took to keep Johnny in cheese sandwiches.

Then came Iowa, which as far as Johnny could remember didn't have a nickname, and eventually, late in the afternoon, there was the Mississippi River. It had been the middle of the night and he had seen nothing but some lights in the water when he had crossed it on the troop train two years before.

Now darkness reappeared, and so did Illinois and his coherence, his sanity as well as his normal feelings as a human being. The hangover was almost over.

As eight o'clock approached, the train slowed through the suburbs toward its final destination at Chicago, where Johnny would switch to a B&O local to Baltimore.

There were reflections once again in a window of a moving train. And there was Betsy. His Betsy.

He relived in full detail every brief moment they had spent together at the Wichita train station.

And he wanted to make up a Dear Betsy that said he had found her again in Wichita.

He wanted to say:

Dear Betsy,

There you were. I had just finished my walk to the semi-pro stadium and was coming back east across the ballpark's parking lot toward downtown. "It's you!" you yelled and ran toward me—freckles and all. "Yes! It's me!" I screamed and ran to meet you. We hugged and kissed and ran our hands over each other's shoulders and faces as if making sure the other was real. "You didn't die after all," you said. "No, and it was because of you," I said. "It's a Miracle Whip," I yelled. "I know you don't know what that means but I'll explain it someday." And so we were married that very afternoon at a brief ceremony in the baseball stadium parking lot. Chapman, my friend the Santa Fe man who'd been in Europe as a P.O.W., was there along with a preacher from that church denomination of yours. We spent our wedding night in my Eaton Hotel room. We did it again, following

our natural instincts again on how to do it. I had never en-
joyed anything as much. You seemed to get a real kick out
of it, too. Then we got on a Santa Fe streamliner for our life
together in baseball.

Oh, Johnny, Oh.

He thought of an O. Henry story he'd read in high school. It was about a man strapped to the electric chair about to be executed for murdering his sweetheart in a jealous rage. And the guy, while waiting for the switch to be pulled, had a dream. He was in a country cottage surrounded by beautiful flowers, his wife, and his little daughter. There was no crime, no trial, no death sentence. This happy man took his wife and kid into his arms. This was the real thing. The awful crime stuff was only a dream. But then the prison warden flipped on the switch. It turned out the guy had dreamed the wrong dream.

The first thing Johnny did at the Chicago train station was buy a pouch of Red Man chewing tobacco.

"COCK-A-DOODLE-DOO," he said, and she repeated after him. They both laughed and hugged each other. And then she let out a holler of joy—and cried her eyes out.

"Cock-a-doodle-doo," their inside jokey line about her store, the Red Rooster, had been Johnny's last words to his mom when he'd gotten on the bus for Baltimore and the marines. Now they were his first upon his return.

A couple of Sylvia Wrigley's friends from the store and Mickey Allen's little sister, Jeannie, were there now with Sylvia at Wilson Rexall, where the bus stopped in Lafayette.

Johnny had given Sylvia only two hours' notice about the homecoming, having telephoned—collect—from a pay phone to announce he would be on the two-fifteen Blue Ridge Motor Coaches bus from Baltimore. Somebody had made a sign on brown wrapping paper that said, WELCOME HOME, OH JOHNNY HERO! Johnny figured Jeannie had done the lettering on paper supplied from the meat department at Sylvia's Red Rooster grocery store.

Johnny was pleasantly surprised at what his two years away had done for Jeannie, whom most everyone around called "Jeannie with the Light Brown Hair"—after the song. She had gone from being a perky tomboy kind of kid who could hit a softball a country mile to a gorgeous knockout who seemed ready for—well, most everything Johnny could imagine a girl could do but play softball. Sylvia called Jeannie a chocolate éclair, and to Johnny's eyes, she was right. Even if it sprung a crack of Betsy guilt through him.

There was another downpour of crying and commotion from Sylvia the next day when a regular customer, a sheriff's deputy named Jerome, said something about how great it was Johnny had made it through the war all right. "Look at him there all freckle-faced and alive like always!"

A couple more days went by before Johnny and Sylvia really talked. That was one night over coffee and apple pie à la mode after work at a little café nearby. There had been so many people, mostly former high school buddies, around that they had not had much time together, just the two of them.

"I had nightmares about you dying, Johnny Oh, I really did," she said. "I wanted to see you in apple pie à la mode dreams coming off the bus all real and alive, wearing a uniform—marine or baseball, it didn't matter. But I never could close my eyes and see you. Never. I figured you must be dead, that's why, and it was just taking the marines a long time to tell me. But I couldn't even see you in a dream lying in white silk in a casket like they did Mickey. So if you were dead like Mickey, where was your body like Mickey's? I was afraid some bomb or something had torn you all up. That kept me awake every night you were gone."

Smithereens was all that was left of his body in his own nightmares as well. And they kept him from sleeping, too. Johnny was glad to hear that there had been enough left of Mickey to lay him out in silk.

Sylvia pulled a small stack of papers from her purse and set them on the purple and white checkered Formica table between them. "These are every letter you wrote me, Johnny." She fingered them, as if counting money at the Red Rooster cash register. "How many would you say there were all together?"

"Not many, I guess," Johnny said.

"Eleven, Johnny. There are eleven. Not even a dozen like what we put in our egg cartons. You were gone more than two years and you wrote me eleven letters. Every day I'd run back to the house during break to get the mail. Every day, Johnny. Only eleven times—not even a dozen eggs times—was there a word, one single word, from my boy, my boy out there in the war. What did you do out there anyhow in the marines?"

"Nothing much, Mom. I'm sorry about the letters. I never have been much of a writer of much of anything."

"You talked about that O. Henry writer all the time."

"Reading what somebody else wrote is a lot different from writing something yourself, Mom."

"I don't have to be told that," Sylvia said. There were tears in Sylvia's eyes now, but at least she wasn't bawling.

"Mom, I really am sorry," he said. "There wasn't much time out there for a lot of letter writing."

"You promise me you'll never do me this way ever again?"

"I promise," said Sylvia Wrigley's only son. He had to fight off a very big laugh at the idea of promising that he would write a lot more letters the next time he went to war with a flamethrower on his back. And all the rest of it.

"Look at this measly one," Sylvia said, pushing a letter toward Johnny.

"I know, Mom. They weren't very long. . . ."

"Just read it. There's more words on a Tootsie Roll wrapper than this."

Johnny unfolded the page of the letter and saw the penciled handwriting he recognized as his own. Big loopy letters, leaning too far to the right—just the way his penmanship had been since he'd first written much of anything, which was in kindergarten.

> *Dear Mom,*
> *I heard Frances Langford sing with Bob Hope. I'm fine.*
> *Johnny*

Johnny handed the letter back to Sylvia and took a big bite of pie. "I was lucky, Mom. That's all that matters now," he said to her.

He mentioned nothing about a connection between his luck in the war and a beautiful chocolate éclair girl at a Kansas train station. He still very much believed that it was his Betsy luck that had saved his life, kept him from being smithereens—like what had happened to Darwin. He couldn't keep from thinking about her occasionally, but there was no point in talking about her to his mom.

He sure as hell wasn't going to tell her about all of those imagined letters he'd written Betsy, some of which were a mile or more long.

Besides, he'd been having a lot of new thoughts about Jeannie Allen with the light brown hair.

AND THE NEXT day Johnny walked the seven blocks to the Methodist parsonage, the two-story white frame house with dark gray shutters where the Allens lived. Paying respects to the Reverend and Mrs. Allen for what had happened to Mickey was the major purpose, but he might have waited awhile longer if it hadn't been for Jeannie Allen. When Johnny had left Lafayette he'd seen Jeannie mostly as Mickey's kid sister who'd had a crush on him in high school, always cheering a little too loudly every time he so much as hit a loud foul ball. Johnny had never made a move in reaction beyond a lot of smiles because not only had Jeannie been Mickey's sister and a preacher's daughter, but she'd been just fifteen years old.

Now she was almost eighteen and somebody very different.

"I really do appreciate you coming to the bus," he said to Jeannie while still standing at the front door. Johnny was really happy that she had been the one to answer his knock.

"Your mom spread the word," said Jeannie. "She was so excited, she could hardly talk."

Johnny heard every word Jeannie said, but it was really hard to concentrate. She had a look on her face that was as good as any he had seen in a movie, not that he'd seen many lately. Her hair was not only a lot like Betty Grable's, but the rest of her—you know, her chest and legs—were in that Ava Gardner wow! category. He couldn't imagine how he could have so completely missed what this girl had had going for her even two years ago.

"Would you like to go to a movie some night?" he asked before he'd really decided to do such a thing. The words just came running out of his mouth like he was a Charlie McCarthy ventriloquist's doll.

"I'd love to," Jeannie said, her face lit up with a smile that was every bit as big and smashing as Betsy's—or Betty's or Ava's. "They're showing *Abilene Town* with Randolph Scott. I remember that Randolph Scott was one of your most favorite movie stars. Isn't that right?"

Johnny was stunned by the coincidence of *Abilene Town* and Randolph Scott. He was about to tell Jeannie that he was no longer interested in seeing Mr. Scott or anybody else in war movies, though. Westerns were fine.

But before he could say anything, Mrs. Allen walked into the front hallway.

She came right over to Johnny and put her arms around him and kissed him lightly on the cheek. "Johnny, Johnny, praise the Lord that at least *you* are safe," she said, her dark brown eyes bright, her graying black hair shiny and, as always, braided so tightly around her head that there was no way to tell how long her hair actually was. Johnny liked Mrs. Allen, even though it always seemed as if most everything about her was wound as tight as her hair.

Johnny knew she was talking about Mickey when she said "you" the way she did. "I am so sorry about Mickey," Johnny blurted out.

"I know, I know," said Mrs. Allen. "But we must always remember that our boy has gone to a better place."

Johnny, in reflex, exchanged looks with Jeannie. He couldn't tell what she was thinking. He knew for a fact that *he* didn't believe being put inside a silk-lined casket and buried in the Maryland dirt was a better place than this parsonage—this town, this anywhere.

The three of them went into the front parlor, where Johnny had spent a lot of time talking and occasionally doing homework or listening to baseball on the radio with Mickey when they weren't actually playing baseball. Mickey had been a second baseman, not anywhere near as good a ballplayer as Johnny but fair in the field, particularly making the double play throw to first. He hadn't been able to hit a curveball, and about the only way he'd ever gotten on base was by running out a bunt, which had been hard for him to do because everyone on the opposing teams had always known that that was what he was going to do.

Johnny accepted Mrs. Allen's offer of a seat on a small couch next to her and across a narrow coffee table from the chair where Jeannie sat down. He also took a glass of iced tea and a peanut butter cookie, which Mrs. Allen said was still fresh, having been baked less than an hour before. Johnny remembered that Mrs. Allen baked something almost every day in case church members happened to drop by the parsonage unannounced, as most did.

"You should know, Johnny, that the service for Mickey was truly special," said Mrs. Allen, once they were settled. "The choir sang that army song about caissons rolling along and 'God Bless America' and four of Mickey's favorite hymns."

Johnny did not take a quick glance at Jeannie this time. But he'd known Mickey better than anybody else in the world, and he was sure Mickey Allen, despite being a preacher's son, had barely known one hymn from another. He always told Johnny he was going to get as far away from "this stuff" as he could the minute the war was over. Mickey had been thinking maybe of even going to college and being something—something different from anybody in Lafayette. Johnny always figured Mickey had meant being a preacher. No way he was ever going to be one of those.

"Reverend Allen spoke at the end, but he did not officiate," Mrs. Allen said to Johnny of Mickey's funeral. "That would not have been appropriate, of course."

"Reverend Allen" was what she always called her husband—Mickey and Jeannie's father. Johnny couldn't remember hearing anybody ever call Reverend Allen by his first name. Sitting there now in the parlor, Johnny wondered if it were possible he didn't even have one? Then Johnny remembered it was Horace, which was good enough reason never to use it.

Johnny couldn't help but think of what Sylvia would have done if a complete body or even just a few smithereens of her son had been brought back to Lafayette. She definitely would have mounted a Methodist funeral, most likely presided over by Reverend Allen. Maybe some of Johnny's ballplayer friends would have carried in the casket, which Johnny hoped wouldn't have been lined in white silk. Maybe something like a marine flag of some kind instead. He knew also that marines in dress blues, like that gunnery sergeant in Wichita, came to the funerals of marines, and saluted or blew bugles. "Bringing in the Sheaves" was the only hymn Johnny really knew well enough to say it was his favorite. If there were music, it would have to include "The Marines' Hymn," which had made Johnny proud and stand straight when he'd heard it in boot camp but not much since. Peleliu and Okinawa were not about music.

"You going to play ball, Johnny?"

Johnny jumped to his feet and turned toward the deep now-for-the-reading-of-the-scripture voice that he immediately recognized as the reverend's.

"Yes, sir, I am," said Johnny.

And there came the Reverend Horace Allen, pastor of the First Methodist Church of Lafayette, Maryland.

"Nobody could play center field like you, young man," said the reverend, a tall rangy man with his blond hair cut in a short flattop. The reverend had chosen not to go into the military during the war, only to wear his hair like those who had. "I join you in thanking the Lord for your gift in the field and at the plate."

Johnny had always heard that the reverend had been a starting pitcher—a left-hander with a tricky changeup—for the Western Maryland State baseball team before he'd found God or something and gone to a seminary. But Johnny had never once seen the reverend even play catch with Mickey. He was always busy doing what Mickey had called "the preacher stuff."

"Would it be appropriate to say a few words now to the Lord about our Mickey?" asked the reverend, grabbing both of Johnny's hands with his own. Mrs. Allen and Jeannie stood, too. All bowed their heads.

"Oh, dear Father of us all, think of our Mickey at this moment as we share our grief with our friend Johnny. We share our belief that God has a plan and that that plan is for all of us to dwell in the house of the Lord forever. Mickey, our son, is already present in the Lord's house. He goes to prepare a place for us all. Thank you, Lord, for doing this for our Mickey. In the name of the Father, the Son, and the Holy Ghost. Amen."

Johnny repeated "Amen." So did Jeannie and Mrs. Allen.

And after he gave a warm, warm smile and a wink, wink, wink, to Jeannie and said his farewells, he walked down the street back home. Johnny couldn't help but wonder if the Reverend Horace Allen was grieving as a father or as a preacher.

Johnny didn't mean anything bad about it. He was just curious how a preacher would separate all of that out.

THEN IT WAS baseball time. Life time, the way Johnny saw it.

Sylvia had always cheered him on to play baseball, but now she made a plea for him to wait awhile. Hang around, take it easy, get your bearings. Maybe take a class at one of the colleges around here—the junior college in Shepstown, even. Work at the Red Rooster part time. Relax.

But Johnny could not wait another minute for baseball. The season was beginning. He was already running late.

Carrying his cleats and glove, and wearing some old jeans and a sweatshirt and cap left over from high school, he put that pouch of Red Man into his pocket and rode the bus over to Shepstown. He knew from the paper that the Bobcats would be playing at home the next seven games.

He arrived ninety minutes before game time. There were players running wind sprints and stretching. He heard them yelling and joking, pounding balls into mitts, hitting flies and ground balls with fungo bats.

This was Johnny Wrigley's world, where he was meant to be.

"I'm here for a tryout," Johnny told a man in a tiny office just off the locker room at the small mostly wooden stadium near downtown. Johnny correctly assumed he was the manager. His name was Rawlins and he was pudgy, tanned, and bald—maybe forty years old.

Without really looking up from the desk, Rawlins said, "We're already set. We don't take walk-ons anyhow. We take what we get from the Tigers' system."

"I'll bet they might have something about me in the Bobcats' files," Johnny said. "They offered me a minor-league Tigers' contract after high school—but I went to war with the marines instead."

The manager looked up. "Everybody went to war with somebody, kid. Even me. Everybody on our team went to war. Don't be thinking you're special."

"I didn't mean that, sir. I'm a ballplayer, that's all. A good one. If you'd just give me a chance to show you what I can do, I think you'll see what I mean."

Rawlins asked for Johnny's name and then went to a drawer in a battered green metal cabinet behind him. He looked through some papers, found something, pulled it out, and gave it a look.

"Yeah, there's an old scouting report in here about you, kid," said Rawlins. "Says you're a center fielder, right-hander— batting and throwing. Can hit short and long, top fielder, fast on the bases, strong arm. Good at the fence."

"That's me, sir," said Johnny.

"Put on your cleats and we'll see for ourselves," said Rawlins, and he then hollered for a coach and a couple of other ballplayers to help him out.

For twenty minutes, Johnny caught fly balls all over the outfield, threw rockets on target to home plate, and hammered pitches low and hard, long and high. All with great energy and hustle.

Johnny could tell right away that the manager was most impressed by him—this kid just out of the marines, just off the train to Baltimore, the bus from Lafayette.

And thus, the dream came true. Johnny Wrigley became a pro, a real baseball player. They gave him a contract to sign, told him to suit up that very evening for the Shepstown Bobcats' Class B Interstate League game against the visiting Wilmington Blue Rocks.

"Is number twenty-seven available, sir?" Johnny asked Rawlins.

"Yeah, I think so. Why?"

"That's Pistol Pete Reiser's number," said Johnny.

Johnny was put in as a pinch hitter in the sixth inning against Wilmington. He hit a curve that banged high on the fence in left, for a stand-up double.

The manager wrote "Wrigley" into the lineup at center field for the next game, and within ten games Johnny was a star—*the* star of the Shepstown Bobcats.

The only problem was that he went off on a road trip with the Bobcats before he got around to taking Jeannie Allen to see *Abilene Town*—or anything else. The fact that he still couldn't get Betsy clear out of his mind probably had something to do with his not finding time for Jeannie.

But Sylvia and Jeannie did make it over from Lafayette to see three of his home games, including the last one against the Hagerstown Suns. Sylvia still didn't own a car, but Reverend Allen let Jeannie drive his old Dodge sedan for the twenty-five-minute drive, each way, from Lafayette to Shepstown and back for day games only.

"For goodness' sake, take that awful tobacco out of your mouth," Sylvia told him after a game. "No girl's going to want to be anywhere near you with that stinking stuff. Right, Jeannie?"

Johnny locked eyes for a second with Jeannie. She had the perfect Betsy-like chocolate éclair smile on her face, which Johnny read as saying that his chewing tobacco wasn't going to be a problem for her.

One of the ballplayers had taken him aside before a game for what he'd called an advanced lesson on how to really chew, which consisted mostly of putting a wad in the side of the mouth between the tongue and cheek, and sucking on it rather than really chewing it. His main advice was to never accidentally swallow the juice because it would make you sick, and always remember to never spit against the wind.

Johnny now turned his head to the side and toward the ground and let go with a squirt of brown spit.

Sylvia frowned, put two fingers to her nose, and said, "Yuck."

Jeannie with the light brown hair lost most of her grin.

And Johnny couldn't help but wonder what his spitting would have done to Betsy's grin.

THE BALL WAS a flaming line drive, a shot to dead center field. Johnny took off at the crack of the bat toward the fence at full speed.

This was a Johnny Wrigley kind of play. His and Pistol Pete Reiser's.

Johnny had had two hits that night—a double into the hole in left and a single on the ground through the box. The chief Detroit scout was in the stands again. Johnny knew from ballplayer scuttlebutt that because of an injury the Tigers needed another outfielder for its Class AA Texas League farm team, the Dallas Rebels. The Texas League, like the Interstate and most of the minors, had just started up again for the 1946 season after having shut down during the war.

Maybe that Tigers scout here tonight meant it was already time to call up this Wrigley kid—the one who was the spitting image of the great Pistol Pete Reiser—if not to the majors at least to AA? It would be most unusual to jump a player from Class B to the majors, but not to AA.

Johnny knew it was coming. If not this year to the big leagues, next for sure. He was hot, and everybody knew it.

After forty-two games Johnny was leading the league in hitting with eighteen home runs, thirty-three runs batted in, and a .345 batting average. He had stolen twenty-two bases, had caught everything that had come his way in center field, and had thrown out almost anyone at home who had had a hope of trying to score from second base on a short single or to stretch a double into a triple.

And now here came that bullet to center. It was a tough play, but one he had made so many times it was now part of his star calling card. He was instinctively certain he had room to race under it and catch it without working up a stretch, a leap, or even a sweat.

It would be the third out. The score would remain Shepstown Bobcats 3, York White Roses 2, going into the last of the eighth. He was second up to bat, one more chance to show that scout and the world of baseball what he could do—how hot he really was.

His mom was there right behind home plate to see her star son do his Miracle Whip thing. She came as often as she could get a ride and when her work schedule at the store permitted.

And the play was going just the way it was supposed to. Johnny easily caught the ball over his left shoulder going away, still running Johnny fast . . .

Crack! Wham!

He felt pain. Everywhere. He hurt everywhere.

He thought of Anderson, the flamethrower assistant, falling from the side of a ship to the bottom of a landing craft.

He had run at full speed into a wall of green concrete.

His Betsy luck had run out.

He was out cold.

JOHNNY SMELLED SOMETHING. Something like medicine. Mercurochrome? His mom used to put it on skinned knees, scratches, nicks, and bites.

If his nose worked, then he was alive. Dead people can't smell.

Unconscious. He must have been knocked unconscious. Out like he'd been from what Jack as in Daniel's had done to him in Wichita.

Now he was beginning to come awake.

He moved his right leg. Then his left. He opened both of his eyes to a squint.

He was alive, all right. He had not been smashed to death against a wall of green concrete.

"Where am I?" he said softly, still groggy.

"You're in the emergency room at the Lady of Good Shepherd Hospital in Shepstown," said a man's voice.

"I'm not a Catholic—or a Lutheran—and she isn't either," Johnny whispered. "She's the religion run by a guy named Heinrich. She isn't Donna Jo Hesston either."

"No need to talk much right now," said the man, whom Johnny still could not see clearly. "You've had quite a hit on your system."

"Two hits. I had two for four tonight—one a double. Her name's Betsy."

"That's good hitting. Betsy must be very proud."

It was not even a vaguely familiar voice. Johnny figured it could have been a ballplayer's. People came and went so fast in baseball it could have been anybody named Slim, Pee Wee, Dizzy, Scooter, Lefty. Baseball, he sometimes thought, was as much about nicknames, statistics, spitting, tiny hotels and rooming houses, and chewing tobacco as it was about anything else. And that was just fine. Everything about baseball was just fine with him. This was his life.

Dear Betsy,
This is my life. I hit two for four tonight.

Johnny closed his eyes again, took a few deep breaths, and remained silent and motionless. He didn't have any idea for how long. A minute maybe. An hour and a mile maybe. That's what his mom used to say about how long it took to make a million dollars, be an all-star—or do or have something valuable like that. It took an hour and a mile, Johnny Oh.

Maybe an hour and a mile later, Johnny could see and think fairly clearly. It brought to mind that kid lieutenant at Peleliu who hadn't quite been able to shake off a daze enough to save his own life.

The emergency room voice wasn't that of Rawlins, the manager, or any other Bobcat. Certainly not that of the Detroit scout. It was a man in a white coat.

"You've got a bad concussion, son," said the man. "And your left arm and shoulder were knocked around quite a bit."

Johnny tried to move his left arm. He couldn't. It was tied down to something. There was a huge white plaster cast on it from the shoulder down to his fingers.

He'd never hurt this much before in his life.

"I gave you some medicine for the pain," said the man. "Unfortunately, the medicine isn't that strong because I want you to come to a bit more."

"You a doctor?" Johnny asked.

"Yes, I am. The name is McPherson. Dr. McPherson."

Johnny felt water rising up toward his eyes. It was the pain, yes. The pain of what had happened to that shoulder and arm but mostly the pain of what had happened to his life.

His Betsy luck had run out. Maybe he should have created a new kind of luck with Jeannie with the light brown hair. He'd seen her several times, but mostly only at the Shepstown ballpark. There had not been time to do any more than that. Whether here or away, he was always playing baseball.

Always playing ball, working his way toward the big leagues.

"GO AHEAD AND cry, Johnny Oh," said Sylvia Wrigley to her son. "What's happened to you isn't going away till the tears come out of you like it does at the Antietam after the spring melt."

Johnny knew what she meant because there had been many April days when they had both watched Antietam Creek rage in near flood stage after heavy winter snows in the Blue Ridge to the west.

But, again, the water wouldn't move on to and out of Johnny's eyes.

Johnny had always been comfortable talking with Sylvia, even if he hadn't been able to get around to it much in letters during the war. Since he was twelve, he had spent as much time at the store with his mom as school and baseball had allowed, helping stack and sack, sweep and wash, and do whatever was needed. They were a family—partners, she called herself and her son, the only ones each other had ever had.

"The future, Johnny. You gotta start thinking about your future," she said after the doctor left her alone with Johnny in the hospital room. "The life of two-inch T-bones and red-pitted olives is over."

Johnny didn't want to yell at her. He had never in his life yelled at her. He did not want to scream that he hadn't cried since Peleliu because he couldn't and, the way things were going, might never again be able to. He didn't want to scream even louder at her that baseball had nothing to do with steaks and fancy foods like olives. It had to do with his goddamn life, which was now in as bad a shape as his left arm and shoulder!

"The future's all I have thought about since I was seven years old," he said as calmly as he could manage. That, she knew, of course, was how old he was when his sonavabitch of a father had left her and him to run away to sea and drown.

"Why did you bring him up to me now?" she said to Johnny, tearless, not even angry. She was just asking.

"I have never brought him up to you," Johnny said.

"You just did. That's what seven years old always means when you say it. Always. It's not my fault he was no good, he was worthless, he didn't care about me or you."

"Hey, Mom, could we do this later? I'm still hurting here a lot."

Sylvia, who was sitting right next to his bed, ignored him completely. She acted as if Johnny had said nothing. "Oh, right, Oh Johnny Oh. Baseball, baseball, baseball," she said. "That's all the future you ever thought about. Now what, Johnny Oh?"

Johnny had barely glanced at her since he'd awoken with her in his hospital room, but he didn't have to see her to know what she looked like. Which was tiny and pretty, tired and spunky. If God had made a plan for her, it stank, it sucked. Personally, at least. She had her grocery store life, but that was about it except for Roger White, the chief butcher at the store who had dated Sylvia off and on for years. She'd also had a fling every once in a while with Stubby Hill, a big baseball nut who worked at the Mack truck dealership in Shepstown.

Jerome, the deputy sheriff, flirted a lot, but it was only one way—him with her.

Johnny knew that his mother had a Crisco lard life in Lafayette, and they both knew there wasn't much either could do about it. Except laugh, which they'd done a lot before he'd told her he was going to be a professional ballplayer and then, when the war came, joined the marines.

"I didn't raise you to die," she had said to Johnny when he'd first mentioned the marines after seeing Randolph Scott in *To the Shores of Tripoli*. But, of course, his friend Mickey had picked the army over the marines, and he was the one who'd died.

"Go to college, Johnny," she said now in the Shepstown hospital room. "You can go to college on the GI Bill. That's what Mickey was going to do. They'll buy your books, pay your tuition, and give you a room—be something besides another Pistol Pete guy you were always talking about."

"I'll be all right," he said. "I'll be back playing ball in no time."

"Yeah, yeah. Until you run into another fence or something. People don't play games for a living, Johnny. They work. Go to college and study how to do something real."

He did not have to tell his mother there had never been anything he'd wanted to study. Everybody in Lafayette High School seemed to know the same amount of stuff—some grammar, math, and biology. Schoolwork itself had never interested him much. The only things Johnny had ever really written for any English class were themes about O. Henry stories. His favorite was a page and a half about "The Gift of the

Magi," the famous O. Henry Christmas love story about the young wife who sold her beautiful long hair to buy her husband a fob for his gold watch. But, as it turned out, the husband had sold the watch to buy his wife some fancy combs for her hair. Both had given up their most prized possession for the other. Johnny had written that it had "the best ending a story could have" and that "only somebody who loved somebody to the hilt" could have written it.

Sylvia Wrigley knew there had never been anything her son had wanted more than just to have a baseball in his hand and nothing he had wanted to be in life besides a baseball player. Not a doctor or lawyer or dentist or businessman or veterinarian or preacher or cowboy or bank robber or anything else.

"You were a marine. Don't you know how to use a gun and things?" she asked. "Be a cop or a deputy sheriff. I know Jerome would put in a good word for you to the sheriff."

Johnny just shook his head. He had never told Sylvia a single thing about what he had done in the marines—what else he had to get over besides his baseball crash. She had asked a few questions about what it had been like for him fighting the Japs and if he'd gotten any medals, but she'd gotten no answers.

He wasn't about to say now that all he'd learned to do really well in the marines was burn people to a crisp with a flamethrower. Not a skill fit for cops or deputy sheriffs.

"How about getting a job at the circus?" she asked.

"The circus?"

Johnny's mom was moving back to being in a joking mood.

That had always been the signal that she was about to go—to go to work, usually.

"Yeah," she said. "Tame lions or tigers, saw women in two, crowd into clown cars—that kind of thing. Step right up to see Oh Johnny Oh!"

He laughed, and so did she like they always did. "Got to run, Johnny. Stubby said he'd give me a ride home. We're open until ten tonight and I haven't got anybody but Roger to close up, and he's so dumb he doesn't even know how to turn out the lights, much less click a padlock shut."

Sylvia kissed her son on the cheek and started to leave.

"Is Jeannie around?" Johnny asked. "I didn't see her."

"That's because she decided that you only had enough time in your life to play baseball and chew tobacco," said Sylvia. "She's all sticky orange marmalade cuddly now on a Cushman motor scooter behind some kid who's learning business math at the junior college."

"Business math?"

"People get paid money by businesses to add and subtract, Johnny Oh," said Sylvia. "It's called working for a living."

She gave him a wave and, again, started to leave.

"Now will you quit chewing that awful tobacco stuff?" she asked.

"Cock-a-doodle-doo, Mom," he replied.

THREE MORNINGS LATER Johnny woke up in his hospital room to find a brown paper bag with his Nocona fielder's mitt, his shined spikes, three meal tickets, and three twenty-dollar bills in it. There was a handwritten note from Rawlins, the Bobcats' manager. "Bad break. Stay in touch." And that was it.

That bag was all Johnny carried with him out of the hospital when he was discharged two weeks after that. The doctor told him to come back in a month so he could see how Johnny was doing.

Not one Bobcat, Tiger scout, or anyone else from his life of baseball, including Rawlins, visited him at the hospital. Johnny understood that they were away on a road trip most of the time and sacked out the rest. Ballplayers are like that. Some of his old high school buddies did come by a few times, and so did a couple of girls—none of them Jeannie with the light brown hair. His mom was right that there just hadn't been enough time to do much else than play ball.

Sylvia came to the hospital most days, coming over and back on the Blue Ridge bus. But the morning he left the hospital she was on duty at the Red Rooster, so he walked out alone. He was intending to pick up his stuff at the rooming house where he'd lived with the rest of the Bobcats and then, probably, just take the bus back to Lafayette.

As he walked, Johnny thought of the worst things that had ever happened to him.

There was Anderson. Peleliu. Darwin burning to death. Those women and children in the Okinawa cave. And before that the kid lieutenant being blown to bits.

Not finding Betsy in Kansas.

Now there was busting himself up playing baseball.

He thought about what he'd say if he were still doing those Dear Betsy letters.

Dear Betsy,

  I'm not done with baseball. I know that. And I know that you know I loved baseball from the time you saw the way I threw that yellow apple.

He thought about his mom's talk about going to college. There were two or three real colleges as well as the junior college in or fairly close to Shepstown. A couple of them even had pretty fair baseball teams. His mom was right about the GI Bill. He'd even heard about a guy who'd bought a house with it.

But if there were two things he did not need right now, it was a house or a college.

What about Betsy? What about trying to get some Betsy luck back?

What about maybe getting on a bus for Kansas?

That dumb thought caused Johnny to laugh out loud—at himself.

JOHNNY WALKED ON down the street from the hospital another few blocks, and there in front of him was the Mack truck place.

Stubby Hill, the sales manager, was a big booster of the Bobcats. He'd had a brief career as a catcher with the Saint

Louis Browns and their San Antonio farm club in the Texas League before the war. Stubby knew his baseball and was known to do some informal scouting for the Browns.

Johnny found Stubby out on the new sales lot between two Mack trucks—a bright red panel and a dark green tractor rig.

"Look at that plaster," Stubby said once he'd focused on the arm. Stubby was a gregarious, loud man—bald, short, and, really, stubby. His face was scarred and his hands were huge and gnarled from wild pitches and collisions at home plate. A perfect catcher specimen with a perfect nickname.

"Oh, Mr. Famous Major-League Catcher Stubby Hill, can I have your autograph on my cast?" Johnny said, and then laughed.

"You bet. Man, man. I heard the sound of your bones cracking way up in the press box the other night when you did that." And Stubby shook his head. "Your mom heard them, too. She was at the game, you know."

Johnny knew that, of course. Stubby had given her a ride from Lafayette to the ballpark that evening in one of his dealership's new pickups. It had been pretty much a date, although as far as Johnny could tell, Stubby had not gone to the hospital with Sylvia once to see Johnny.

"Don't say it's over for me, Stubby," Johnny said.

"I'm not saying anything, kid. To you or to your mom. Pistol Pete always comes back. So can you."

Pistol Pete Reiser, back with the Dodgers after the army, had picked up right where he'd left off, hitting and running the bases at a league-leading pace. And running into fences. Johnny had seen it in the sports pages. Pete had knocked himself out twice already that Johnny had read about. Once, it said in the papers, they brought a Catholic priest out to center field to administer Pete his last rites, they were so worried he wouldn't make it.

It made Johnny think that the Methodists probably didn't have a last rites kind of thing they could give him after running into a center field fence. If it ever seemed almost necessary— again.

"Did the Bobcats release you?" Stubby asked Johnny.

"Yeah," Johnny said. "Kind of. For now, at least."

"You staying around? Or going on off somewhere?" Stubby asked.

Johnny, thinking while he was talking, realized there really was no reason to hang around Shepstown *or* Lafayette. Everywhere Johnny'd go, people would want to know how Johnny Wrigley, Lafayette's big baseball star of past and future, had smashed himself up, and they'd ask if he was going to have to quit playing ball. . . . No, thanks. When he'd first gotten home from the marines, there'd been so many questions. Had he won any medals? And why not? Mickey had. They'd given 'em to his mom and dad after he'd died. How many Japs did you kill, Johnny? Did you meet General MacArthur? Did you see the A-bomb explode? Did Patton slap you, too?

But Johnny had no other place to go. Kansas definitely was a laugh idea, no matter his Betsy luck problem.

This was it for him.

Johnny told Stubby he was thinking he would stay in Shepstown—for just a few weeks maybe while his arm and shoulder healed. He could get a job and start getting ready to play ball again.

"Maybe I can play some semi-pro ball while I'm getting back in shape," Johnny told Stubby.

"Yeah, sure, Johnny Oh. There are more than a couple of semi-pro teams around Baltimore, I know," Stubby said. "They run a national tournament for their championships in some place in Kansas or Missouri, I think."

Johnny let that go. He did not say that he knew exactly where the semi-pro championships were played. He had, in fact, been to the stadium. It was definitely not in Missouri. That was the Show-Me State. Wichita was in Kansas, the Sunflower State, the home of much more than a baseball stadium.

"You got a place to live, so you're set, then?" Stubby asked.

"Right. That rooming house over on Hanover Street. But the team may not let me stay there now without paying . . ."

"Well, great, then. Good luck. Got a customer to see about a truck."

Great, then, good luck? Johnny might have expected Stubby to give him a real hand. Ask maybe if he needed some money or some other help, like maybe even with finding a temporary job. That kind of help is what he had always been told baseball people did for one another.

"You haven't got something around here a one-armed

ballplayer could do for a while?" Johnny pressed, looking around the truck lot. "I'm going to need a job while I get back together to play ball."

"Sorry, Johnny. We're overstaffed now already with all the vets we *had* to take back. You know, they worked here before the war and we had to give their jobs back when they got out."

Yeah, Johnny knew.

"Stay in touch, Johnny Oh," said Stubby as he turned his attention back to a new Mack truck.

OH, JOHNNY, OH.

As he walked slowly away from Stubby and his Macks, Johnny thought about how he liked being called Johnny Oh. Several of the Bobcats had begun to do it. Earlier, Mickey and the guys in high school had, too. Johnny saw that as a great nickname for when he got into the majors. Johnny Oh Wrigley, as in Joltin' Joe DiMaggio. Pistol Pete Reiser.

Also, as in the way he had signed off some of his Dear Betsys. Johnny Oh. He so much at this moment wanted Betsy to sing a song to him—any song. Or say a word to him that would make it all better. Wouldn't it be the best thing in his life if Betsy sang "Haunted Heart"? Think about what that would be like for him—particularly right now.

Besides the three twenties in his pocket, he had forty-five dollars to his name, four tens and a five that he kept hidden in his pillowcase back in his room. Most of that was left over from his mustering-out pay from the marines after he had bought a new pair of cleats that, along with his mitt, were in the paper bag he was carrying. The Bobcats had paid him barely enough money to stay even, after buying cigarettes, having cheese sandwiches, or having an occasional hamburger steak dinner away from the group team meals.

Johnny's room was not much bigger than a ballpark dugout. There was barely enough space for a single bed and a table that had a tiny lamp on it that put out less light than a refrigerator with the door open. The bathroom was down the hall and had to be shared with the ballplayers and about ten other men roomers of various ages and smells. Johnny thought of it all as a furnished room, as in "The Furnished Room," one of O. Henry's saddest surprise-ending stories. Johnny didn't bother to remember all of the details because it was so sad. It was about how young lovers ended up separated in the big city and then, weeks apart and unbeknownst to each other, committed suicide separately in the same bed by opening the gas jets in the same furnished room. A real downer.

He tried to switch to thinking like a marine.

Don't let the bastards get you down. Never give up. The difficult will be done immediately; the impossible will take a little longer. Semper Fi, gung ho, and all that crap. Yeah, yeah, yeah. What would Chesty Puller do—no, not him. He got half his regiment wiped out on Peleliu. Darwin's death wasn't Puller's fault. Or maybe it was. Maybe if Puller had done his job leading his regiment better, Darwin wouldn't have become separated from his unit. . . .

That made Johnny think again, for the ten thousandth time, what an incredible Miracle Whip it was that he not only hadn't died but had barely gotten a scratch.

But if he couldn't play baseball, then what was the point? Without Betsy either? What was the point of not dying?

There on the corner on his left he saw the Blue Ridge Motor Coaches bus depot.

Think of Shepstown as Okinawa. Get the hell off this island—out of this town.

Baltimore. Yeah. Go to Baltimore—at least to Baltimore, if not Kansas. It's a real city with lots of jobs to do, lots of people.

Baltimore was also where his lousy dad had run off to.

Maybe it runs in the family like freckles.

Oh, Johnny, Oh.

THERE WAS AN hour to wait for the next Baltimore bus. Johnny had thrown his stuff into his duffle, gotten out of his room, and gone into the Burnside Tavern, named for some Civil War general, a couple of blocks from the bus depot. It had a half dozen booths and ten seats at the bar, its walls covered with Civil War photos and posters, and a few lighted signs for various beers. There was the smell of beer and cigarettes and onions frying.

Johnny had never been in a real tavern—beer joint—like this before. That little place at the Wichita hotel definitely didn't count. He took a seat at the bar and ordered a Jack as in Daniel's from the bartender, who, from the looks of him, was a vet. Probably navy, about thirty years old, almost no hair. His short-sleeved shirt showed off big muscles decorated with tattoos about mother, America, and "Ralph." Johnny assumed the bartender was Ralph, and the guy confirmed it when Johnny asked, the first thing he did once at the bar.

"You twenty-one, kid?" Ralph said to Johnny.

Johnny pointed at the cast on his left arm and shoulder. "I know some Japs who'd think I was a lot older than that."

"On the rocks, with soda, water—how do you want it?" said Ralph with a brand-new smile.

Johnny had heard from some of the ballplayers that vets got served whatever, whenever, and wherever they wanted. A Bobcats shortstop had told him that was the way it was in America, and there wasn't a cop from sea to shining sea who'd ever do anything about it.

"No ice. Nothing else, thanks. Just the whiskey," Johnny said.

A glass with three inches of Jack Daniel's bourbon was set before him.

At first, Johnny was afraid the bartender—Ralph—would now ask him about the Bobcats, the crash into the center field fence. But Ralph didn't say a word about the Bobcats. Maybe he'd ask about the war. What branch of service? Where had Johnny been? How had he hurt his shoulder? How had the Japs done it to him? But, thank God, Ralph asked not a question.

Johnny had not had even a sip of anything alcoholic, including beer, since that calamity at the Eaton Hotel in Wichita. He had sworn it off for baseball and for the rest of his life. And, without ever saying so, for Betsy. There'd never been a mention of drinking, not even smoking, in any Dear Betsy.

Now Johnny emptied the glass in a flash. He moved his head to ask for another and Ralph came back with a bottle. "You sure?" he asked.

"I'm sure, yes, sir."

"You going on the bus?" the tattooed man named Ralph asked while pouring Johnny another drink.

"That's right. To Baltimore. I'm a ballplayer." Johnny downed almost half of the second glass in just a couple of swallows.

"Be careful, then, kid. Some of these bus drivers won't let people with too much drink in 'em ride the bus. Worried about people peeing in their pants or barfing on the passengers."

Johnny nodded, and then asked, "You happen to have a calendar I could look at?"

Ralph produced a folded calendar off the back of the bar. There was a page for every month, the days laid out in squares. The calendar advertised Falstaff beer, and there were colored photos of deer, moose, and other wildlife on the top of each page.

Johnny folded the calendar to April. He pointed to the square for the fourteenth. April fourteenth. "That was the day in 1944 when I left Betsy," he said to the bartender and the couple of others who were sitting at the bar. Nobody seemed to notice either Johnny or what he was saying.

"I think it's time for your bus, kid," the bartender said after the rest of the second glass of whiskey was gone.

"I know," Johnny said, paying for his two glasses of Jack Daniel's. "I'm a ballplayer, Ralph."

"Everybody's a ballplayer when they're at a joint like this, kid," said Ralph the bartender.

JOHNNY PUT TWO nickels into the pay phone and told Sylvia he had only a minute before his bus came.

"I'm going to Baltimore, Mom," he said.

"You been drinking?" Sylvia responded almost before he'd finished the sentence.

"I'll stay in touch. I promise," he said.

"Like all those letters you wrote in the war?"

"Cock-a-doodle-doo, Mom."

"Don't you cock-a-doodle-doo me, young man. What did you do in the war, anyhow? I'm beginning to think it was a worse Crisco lard for you than you ever said."

Johnny, without a thought, said, "I wore a flamethrower on my back."

"Oh, Johnny! No! Those awful things. I saw them shooting all that fire in the newsreels. . . ."

"I hear the bus now, Mom. I'll write you a letter."

"No, you won't!"

And Johnny hung up and made a dash for the bus.

JOHNNY THOUGHT AT first that he might have some trouble with the bus driver. The smell of Jack as in Daniel's and the slight staggering made it pretty obvious what Johnny'd been doing at Burnside.

"You get sick on me, boy, and I'll put you off this bus along the side of a country road in the middle of nowhere, or right in front of the next police station," said the driver at the bus door.

"There won't be a problem, sir, I promise," said Johnny.

"No 'sirs' here. I was enlisted," the driver said. He tore off the main part of the ticket, punched it three times with a hand punch, and gave the receipt part to Johnny.

The driver gestured with his head toward the cast on Johnny's shoulder and arm. "Run into a girl or a door—or a Jap?"

Johnny shrugged but did not answer. Questions. No questions, please. Just take me to Baltimore/Kansas!

Unlike the old Kansas Central driver, there was a definite military style about this Blue Ridge guy. He was a trim man in his thirties dressed sharply in his two-tone gray uniform and black shoes. The uniform was in full starch and crease, and the shoes had been something close to spit shined. There was a two-inch silver badge on the driver's cap that had a blue bus in the center and the shape of mountains, presumably the Blue Ridge, behind it. The number thirty-seven was engraved at the bottom.

As Johnny made a move to board the bus, the driver said, "Hold on there a minute. I'll take care of your stuff—put it in the baggage compartment underneath."

Johnny was grateful. It really was hard to handle it all with one arm. The driver was looking hard at Johnny's olive drab canvas duffle bag, which he was carrying in his left hand. Johnny had retrieved it from his room before going to the bar. Inside that duffle was everything he owned except his old marine uniforms, which he'd left at his mom's house when he'd gone off to play ball.

"You were a marine?" asked the driver with a very big smile.

Then Johnny realized what had caught the man's eye. Stenciled on the bag in black on the side in inch-high letters was WRIGLEY, J.C., and directly below was USMC.

"I was, yeah," said Johnny.

The driver stuck out his right hand. "Semper Fi. Take that front seat up there across from mine. We call it the angel seat. It's for beautiful women, marines, and other angels."

It was the first time Johnny had had a happy feeling about anything in the two weeks and three days since he'd gone for that flaming line drive toward dead center field.

They talked quite a bit over the next two hours of the ride into Baltimore, including over a grilled cheese, french fries, and cherry Coke lunch that the driver insisted on buying for Johnny during a rest stop at Frederick. His name was Nick Didden. He'd been with Blue Ridge before the war, and, like the good Santa Fe man in Wichita, his employers had not only given him his job back but with the accumulated seniority for when he'd been away in the service. That was why he could bid and hold such a daylight run as this from Pittsburgh to Baltimore.

Johnny, sobering up, told him about crashing into the center field wall. And that, like a fool, he had now simply gone off on this bus to Baltimore or wherever without a job or anything else going for him except a hope that someday he'd heal enough to play ball again.

"You're going to be fine," Nick said.

You're going to be fine.

Johnny had the strange feeling that Nick was reciting those words from memory like Miss Lytton had everybody do poetry. It made Johnny consider that Nick might have had dreams about being something other than a bus driver. Most everybody dreams big to begin with. Johnny's own problem was a lot like the guy's in the O. Henry story who'd dreamed the wrong dream. Maybe the bus driver had, too?

Johnny talked with the driver about Pete Reiser. Nick argued that he was the best in the majors except for Joltin' Joe DiMaggio. Johnny reluctantly agreed. Then they went through the prospects this year in both the American and National leagues. Nick was a New York Yankees fan, something Johnny found unimaginable. As one of the pitchers at Shepstown had said, being for the Yankees was like rooting for the king against the peasants.

It was only as the bus was pulling into the big depot in Baltimore that Johnny realized that they had not talked about the marines and the war. Neither had ever asked a question of the other about where exactly he'd served or what he'd done.

The closest they'd come to the subject had been when the bus had gone past the Antietam battlefield and crossed the small bridge over Antietam Creek at Sharpsburg. The water had been summer shallow, quiet, peaceful.

Nick had said, "I had driven by this place hundreds of times and never known what it was really all about. I do now."

Johnny, briefly telling Nick about his own school trip there, had said, "Me, too."

And at Baltimore, Nick told Johnny, "Stay on the bus and ride over to the Blue Ridge garage with me. Let's see what we can do about finding you a job."

When Johnny made a mild protest, Nick said, "There are things even busted-up ballplayer marines can do in the bus business, Johnny."

One of them, it turned out, was working on the wash rack, cleaning the buses between runs. It takes only one arm to point a big water hose at the side of a dirty bus. The guy in charge, on Nick's recommendation alone, hired Johnny on the spot.

"We've got a semi-pro team called the Blue Ridge Drivers," said Nick. "Most of the players are ringers—ex-pros like you—so who knows what might happen."

What he would have said in a Dear Betsy was that he had met a very nice man, also a former marine, who had all the signs of becoming a very good friend.

AND, BELIEVE IT or not, he wrote his mother a letter, the longest real one he had ever written to her—or to anyone else.

Dear Mom,

See this? I promised you I would write and I have done it. Aren't you sorry now you didn't believe me? I'm doing just fine. That's the important thing I have to say. I got a job with the Blue Ridge bus people that keeps me out and about and gives me enough money to buy a cheese sandwich or a choco-late éclair when I want one. No tobacco. Seriously, no Red Man, not now. Maybe that is the biggest news of all. The rea-son is that there's no point in chewing if I'm not playing ball. Maybe I'll start up again when I go back to center field. I know that's going to happen someday. Count on it. I know you want me to start thinking about doing something else, and maybe I will. But my arm and shoulder are already feel-ing better. Another reason for not chewing is that I've started dating a girl. She works here at Blue Ridge, too. I don't think my chewing would have bothered Jeannie, but this new girl I'm not sure. Have you heard anything more about Jeannie, by the way? The new girl's name is Rose. Nick, a bus driver who drove me into Baltimore, helped me find a room to rent with another driver's sister's family less than ten blocks from the Blue Ridge garage. It's three times the size of that place back at Shepstown, has a large double bed, and it's got flowered wallpaper and sheets. Really cheerful. Nothing like that room in the O. Henry story I told you about. That's it for now. Cock-a-doodle-doo, Mom.

Johnny Oh

Rose's last name was DeCarlo. She was a clerk in the maintenance supervisor's office at the garage. Compared to Betsy with her reddish brown curls or Jeannie with the light brown hair—no, he really had to stop doing that. The fact was that Rose was pretty—in her own way. Her eyes were dark brown, almost black, and her hair was as black as school ink. It all went with being Italian, as did her silky olive skin. And she was smaller than the others—"petite" was probably the word to describe her size. "Lively," "peppy" were the words that fit her personality. She sparkled. Most important, she seemed to take instantly to Johnny, who thought it was possible Nick had put her up to it, but he never asked because he didn't want to know. Whatever was behind it, Johnny didn't have to do any heavy courting. Her smiles and her body twists and turns extended the first invitation to just take a walk down to the harbor.

Johnny and Rose took many strolls and drank Cokes together and went to movies, including, even, *Abilene Town.*

Randolph Scott was as good as he'd ever been. But Johnny was careful to always deflect any suggestion from Rose that they go to a war movie. He had loved them before he was actually in a real war. Now he saw them as bad jokes. Bible war movies, George Washington war movies, Civil War movies, World War One movies, our war movies. They want people at home to think it's all clean. No bodies blown to smithereens. No women and children fried. It's all neat little bullet holes through the heart. It hurts, but only for a while, only long enough for the movie marine or rebel or Union soldier or gladiator to say he loves his girl or his momma or his America.

Rose lived in Little Italy, which was only a couple of blocks farther south and east from the bus garage and Johnny's place. They weren't able to go out too much during the week because Rose was going to a business school at night to learn shorthand, typing, and other skills that would lead to her being a real secretary.

Johnny had trouble at first making out with Rose. Every time he hugged or kissed her, he felt he was being disloyal to Betsy. A couple of times Johnny was sure Betsy, from somewhere out there in Kansas, was watching. Once, after a particularly heavy petting session with Rose, he even imagined an angry Betsy threw a rock—something much harder than a baseball—at his head. She missed.

Meanwhile, Johnny thoroughly enjoyed what he and Rose were doing. Some of the playing around happened out in front of people on park benches or, even, while walking along the streets of Baltimore. But as it got heavier, they found more private spots in various places around his rooming house and, a couple of times, in the backseats of empty Blue Ridge buses.

He hadn't completely ruled out the possibility that maybe someday there would be an extreme recurrence of his Betsy luck that would bring her into his life. But for now, life had to go on without Betsy and with Rose. Betsy luck was thus replaced by Betsy guilt.

Everything quickened and intensified, in more ways than one, after Rose let him put a hand up her skirt, keep it there, and move it around awhile. It happened in the Blue Ridge parking lot in the back of a new ACF Brill Silversides.

That led to their first really big date. They went for Saturday night dinner to Ricardo's, one of scores of family-owned Italian restaurants and grocery stores in Little Italy. Rose's dad was the head waiter at Ricardo's, where he had worked for thirty years or more. The dinner was his treat.

And it was indeed a real treat for Johnny, who had never been to what would be called a serious sit-down restaurant with such things as white cloth tablecloths, red wine, heavy salt and pepper shakers, and waiters who wore black bow ties and white shirts.

Then, after they had joyfully consumed a full array of bread sticks, salads, pasta and veal, hot cheese-flavored bread, and vanilla and cherry cannoli, Rose's dad joined them at the table. He was short like his daughter but also stocky and bald like Stubby Hill.

After only a few preliminaries, Mr. DeCarlo got down to business with Johnny.

"I know you're not Italian or Catholic, right?" Mr. DeCarlo asked the question with less feeling than he would have brought to taking a customer's order of spaghetti and meatballs.

"Not really a practicing one," Johnny said.

"What does that mean? You're either Catholic or Italian or you're not. What's there to practice?"

Johnny could see red creeping through the olive in Rose's face. And it only got worse.

"I hear you were a marine in the war, right?" asked Mr. DeCarlo. Johnny didn't see a written list of questions in front of the man, but he definitely had worked on this routine.

Johnny nodded.

"Honorable discharge, I can only assume, right?"

Johnny nodded.

"My brother's wife's cousin's son was a marine," Mr. DeCarlo said. "He died at Guam."

Johnny was tempted—only for a stupid passing second—to say something like, "Well, I was at Peleliu and Okinawa, and I was about the only marine there who *didn't* die. Would you say that was too bad?"

But he said nothing.

Mr. DeCarlo moved on to, "You plan to make a career washing buses?"

Johnny said, "It's a job, and I need a job. That's all I know now. I'm a ballplayer."

"You hurt yourself playing ball?"

"That's right."

"Never hear much about baseball players getting hurt bad. It's usually the football players. Or boxers."

Johnny had no answer to this. Obviously, Mr. DeCarlo didn't follow baseball well enough to know about Pistol Pete Reiser of the Brooklyn Dodgers. Or Johnny Oh Wrigley of the Shepstown Bobcats. Baseball players who play hard get hurt, too.

"You thinking about going to school like Rose?" Mr. DeCarlo persisted. "There are lots of really good jobs out there for men with schooling, you know. You could do it on the GI Bill, like a lot are doing. You can buy a house on that, too."

At that moment, Rose's mother appeared at the table. To Johnny's eyes she was a female equivalent—physically, at least—of the man she had married. Except she wasn't bald.

Johnny knew now that the evening had been an old-fashioned setup. The DeCarlos were thumping the tires of the man their pretty, perky little daughter, no doubt very much against her parents' wishes, was thinking about marrying. It was not until right then, sitting in this restaurant, that the idea of marrying Rose even crossed Johnny's mind. She was a nice girl and he enjoyed being with her and enjoyed her spirit, but that was all. For right now, at least.

Johnny paid little attention to much of anything that was said after Mrs. DeCarlo took a seat. He could hear her talking, along with her husband and daughter occasionally, but he wasn't listening.

This was getting way, way too complicated. Not even a writer as good as O. Henry could have told this in a way that made sense—that worked. Who would read a story about a flamethrowing banged-up ballplayer who'd had his life changed forever by a few minutes with a beautiful girl during a troop train stop in Kansas? And now couldn't find her so he went for the first girl he met and the first good meal he was offered?

This story needed an ending. Maybe even a *surprise* ending? Most of O. Henry's were happy. But not all of them.

After they said good night to her parents at the restaurant, Johnny took Rose back to his room and his bed.

Based on what had come naturally that one time at the train station, Johnny did with Rose what he had done with Betsy, only it lasted a lot longer this time.

And it kept alive his thoughts and his guilt about Betsy.

ONE MORNING JOHNNY got called off the wash rack.

"Telephone for you, Wrigley!" one of the crew chiefs yelled. "She said it was long distance. It'd better be important. We've got an express and three locals lined up out there."

Johnny had never gotten a long-distance phone call—important or otherwise. He figured somebody must have died.

"Cock-a-doodle-doo, Johnny Oh," said Sylvia Wrigley.

Her voice was full of joy. Clearly, nobody had died.

"What's up, Mom? I'm right in the middle of something right now—"

"You did it, Johnny Oh! You promised you would, and you did!"

Johnny still didn't get it. "What are you talking about? Is everything all right?"

"I got a letter from you this morning. It came in the morning mail. It's a long letter, Johnny Oh. Longer than any you ever wrote. Cock-a-doodle-doo!"

"Cock-a-doodle-doo," he responded. He was smiling.

"You're not thinking about marrying this Rose girl you wrote about, are you?" Sylvia asked.

"Hey, Mom, I gotta go back to work."

"Check it out some more. The beach is full of pebbles. Jeannie might get interested again. There are a lot more out there for you to choose from, Johnny Oh. Hope you're still not chewing that awful yuck stuff. Is Rose Catholic? You're not, you know."

"You're a real apple pie à la mode, Mom," he said.

"So are you, Johnny Oh. Thanks for the great letter. Got to run."

And they both hung up.

PROVIDING HIM WITH his first full-scale sex experience was not the only important thing Rose did for Johnny. Through a friend who was a nurse's aide at a big hospital in Baltimore named Johns Hopkins she helped him find a doctor who specialized in Johnny's kind of injury.

The doctor was Jerry Mann, an orthopedic surgeon who had been an army doctor in the war.

Mann was funny, smart, and pessimistic when he first examined what had been under Johnny's plaster cast.

"How did you do this, run as fast as you could into a wall?" he asked.

"Yes, as a matter of fact," replied Johnny. "You got to fix it so I can play ball again, Doctor."

"I'm but a simple surgeon god, not a miracle man."

Johnny considered making a Miracle Whip crack of some kind but decided he wasn't ready for a joke right then.

He read what was in the frames on the doctor's office wall. Mann had graduated from the University of Texas, another college, named Brown, as well as from here, the Johns Hopkins medical school. He had been a major in the U.S. Army medical corps and had graduated from army paratrooper and ranger schools, too. Some guy. If not a Miracle Whip man.

He had an accent that was similar to Darwin's, and he stood at least six feet tall. A long white coat had him pretty much under cover, but Johnny figured there was likely to be very little fat in his body.

And the doctor knew his baseball. He even had a ball on his desk that Joe DiMaggio had autographed when their paths had crossed in the army.

"You're in worse shape, I think, than even Pete Reiser," the doctor said to Johnny.

Johnny was impressed that a doctor knew about his hero. And he told Mann so.

"Pete keeps coming back—so far, at least," the doctor said. "I'm not sure there's any way *you're* going to catch another fly ball or swing a bat with this abomination of an arm and shoulder the way they are now, Johnny."

Then he slowly raised up Johnny's left arm as far as it would go. Which wasn't halfway between his waist and his head.

And it hurt like hell to go that far. Johnny had to fight off a real shriek of pain.

"Let's try it again," said the doctor.

This time Mann moved the arm up a little faster. Which caused it to hurt a little more.

And he did it again and again. Each time, while the pain grew, so did the distance he could raise it. Only an inch or so more each time, but that was progress.

"We can make some headway with some heavy-duty physical therapy, but I don't know how far we can go with that, Johnny. I'm going to send you down for some X-rays. How important is it that you play ball again?"

"No more important than breathing, sir."

"I assume you were in the war. What did you do?"

"I was a marine, sir."

"What kind of marine?"

Questions. Why did everybody keep asking him questions? "The alive kind, sir."

Dr. Jerry Mann laughed. It was genuine, but it was also clear to Johnny that Mann knew there was more to that quip than a laugh.

"You okay up here about the war?" Dr. Mann asked Johnny, thumping his head with a finger.

Nobody had ever asked Johnny such a question. Not even Nick. Most everybody asked vets what they'd done but not how they felt about it afterward. Without a thought, he just shrugged. That was his answer.

The doctor said: "I saw a guy stand up in the middle of a heavy firefight in France, throw down his M1, scream something about screwing Betty Grable on top of his grandma's Ping-Pong table in Grand Rapids, Michigan, and take off running right into the Nazis' fire. He was cut in two. I mean, right in two. The top part of his body was separated from his bottom half by machine-gun fire almost as neat and tidy as if it had been done with a hatchet. A colonel—must have gone nuts, too—ordered me and another doctor to tie the poor dead bastard's two halves back together. We couldn't, of course. I wondered what they told his family about how he'd died. I hope they didn't tell the truth. 'Hey, your son cracked up so bad he got himself killed intentionally.' "

When Johnny didn't say anything, he and Jerry Mann went back to talking about getting Johnny fixed up so he could play baseball again.

AND OVER THE next several weeks, Johnny, under the guidance of Dr. Mann, gave everything he had, physically and spiritually, to bringing his left arm and shoulder back to life.

Before going to the Blue Ridge garage, Johnny came to the

physical therapy room at Johns Hopkins every morning at six-thirty. He spent an hour doing exercises, lifting weights, and whatever else the therapist, a returned navy corpsman, told him to do.

The first big day came when Johnny showed up for a routine visit to Mann's office and the doctor pulled a Louisville Slugger baseball bat from behind his desk. "Surprise, Mr. Wrigley," he said, handing it to Johnny. "Let's see if you can hold it and swing it. Look out for the furniture."

Johnny recognized the clean, full, strong signature at a glance. It was a Pete Reiser bat! It had Pistol Pete's autograph engraved into the wood up on the barrel of the bat. All Louisville Sluggers had major leaguers' names on them. Johnny had seen it etched on many gloves as well as bats. Johnny, in fact, had even tried to copy Pete's rounded style of penmanship in writing his own name. He'd practiced it several times on pages of notebook paper so his autograph would be ready when they put out signed versions of Johnny Wrigley bats and gloves.

Not bad, Johnny had thought at the time.

Johnny now held the Pete Reiser bat like it was a piece of gold. He took it by the handle with his good right hand and then slowly moved his left arm around so he could get a grip. He lowered the bat down in front of him and then moved it back between his legs as if he were waiting to raise it up over his right shoulder to take a pitch.

Mann clapped his hands together. "Well done. Now see if you can go the whole way."

There were twinges of pain and discomfort but Johnny got the bat up there over his right shoulder.

And he went into his stance, bending his legs slightly, leaning down a bit and peering to his left as if waiting for the pitcher to deliver the ball.

"Swing the bat," Mann said. "Gently, ever so gently, for Christ's sake—but swing it."

Johnny brought the bat back in the slight hitch that had always been part of his swing, and then glided the bat down and in front of him as if going for a pitch down the middle.

Two weeks later, in Dr. Mann's office, he tried to lift his left arm up high over his head where it needed to be if he was ever again going to catch a high fly ball going away.

"It's never going to get much better than this, Johnny," said the doctor. "There will always be weakness and vulnerability."

"Can I play ball again?"

Dr. Mann shook his head. "Not the pros."

"Semi-pro?"

The doctor shrugged. "Why not? If you're up to trying."

"I am," Johnny said, staring at the doctor's Joe DiMaggio–autographed baseball while thinking of Kansas.

JOHNNY SHOWED UP at Mencken Field with the new Pete Reiser bat, his mitt, his cleats—and his life.

His fielder's mitt, given to him by Sylvia on his fifteenth birthday, was a regulation glove made by a famous Texas company called Nocona. The leather was an orangy tan, except in the pocket, which was dark with heavy rubbings of neat's-foot oil, the magic substance ballplayers everywhere used to keep the leather limber and free from cracking. Johnny had heard somewhere that the oil came from boiling the feet and shinbones of cattle, but what mattered to him was that it had an odor of peanuts that was the smell of baseball.

Johnny's cleats, called spikes by some ballplayers, were the standard three-prong metal ones stapled firmly on the heels and toes of black leather-topped shoes. He'd bought his pair new with his mustering-out pay from the marines. Keeping the tops shined and the cleats clean was critical, a task that had come to Johnny naturally and obsessively even before he'd been a marine.

He was so nervous now, so anxious, that on the transit bus ride over he didn't even try to bring Betsy's face to mind. He didn't want her to see him like this.

Mencken Field, in northeast Baltimore, was the Blue Ridge Drivers home field, where they practiced and played many of their games. Johnny figured Mencken was the name of somebody local because he knew of no major-league baseball player named Mencken. It was hardly a stadium—as in not like that big semi-pro field in Wichita or even the Shepstown or the others in the Interstate League. This field was mostly two sets of unpainted slat bleachers on either side of a baseball diamond. But, to Johnny's view, the field was full regulation size and very well cared for, the infield dirt being level and raked, the infield and outfield grass cut.

A chain-link fence surrounded it on three sides, with a tall heavy wood section in center field that was painted green.

That green part was the first thing Johnny really saw. That was where it was going to happen or not happen for him. Out there in center field in front of that green wall was where he was going to find out about his life from here on. That's where he'd know if he was ever going to be any kind of ballplayer again. Even just a semi-pro.

Johnny had called the manager, told him he was a center fielder who had played Class B ball with Shepstown, and asked if he could come for a tryout. The manager, whose named was Lefty Oliphant, had said the team was pretty set but there was no harm in coming by Saturday morning about eleven. They'd be having a practice before getting on a bus to play a game that night down in Glen Burnie. Lefty made it more than clear that he was doing this because somebody at Blue Ridge Motor Coaches had done some leaning on him. Nick had told Johnny he was going to get one of the company executives to make a call.

The Drivers were doing well this season. Johnny knew that from what he heard around the garage but also from reading the sports sections of the Baltimore newspapers, which he had always devoured—particularly during baseball season. That was how he had found out so much about Pete Reiser, including the time Reiser had almost died from banging into the wall in Brooklyn.

The Blue Ridge team was leading their semi-pro league and had a good chance of going further into the regional and maybe even the national play-offs. The *national* play-offs!

Those were the ones played in Wichita, Kansas. *The* Wichita, Kansas.

The players were taking batting and infield practice now. They were in their visiting team gray flannel uniforms that were as good as any pro team's, trimmed in blue with "The Drivers" written in script on the front. Their blue caps had embroidered replicas of the metal badge Nick and the real Blue Ridge drivers wore on their uniform caps.

It took a minute for Johnny to see that Nick had had it right about the Drivers. These were not a bunch of bus workers who played pickup game baseball for fun. Many of them clearly had pro or some other kind of real baseball experience, the way they swung the bat, made throws around the infield. He reminded himself again that Pistol Pete himself and many other stars had played for semi-pro military teams. Although the big names had now gone back to the majors or AAA minors, this was still a place where real baseball was played. A Blue Ridge bus big shot could get him a tryout, but there was nothing he could do to help Johnny win a place on this ball team.

And that was just fine with Johnny. It had to be that way if it was going to work—*really* work.

Lefty Oliphant was fat, of course. What was it that turned skinny left-handed pitchers and right-handed first basemen, among others, into butterballs once they became managers?

"Why don't you take some swings?" Those were the first words Lefty said, once Johnny came all the way onto the field and made his presence known. Hitting first made perfect sense to Johnny. If a ballplayer can't swing the bat, it doesn't matter much what he can do in the field. He thus knew that if he didn't hit well, he'd never get a chance to see what would happen out there in front of the green fence in center.

Johnny was aware of the stares he was getting from the players as he put on his spikes. It was like the Shepstown tryout all over again. He knew what the others saw was a guy in a dark blue T-shirt and faded jeans who thought he was a ballplayer. Poor kid. Look at him there, about to make a goddamn fool of himself in front of all us great ballplayers. . . .

Johnny took his Pete Reiser bat and walked into the batting

cage at home plate, scuffed some dirt around with his cleats, and went into his stance.

The pitcher, a plump right-hander, yelled, "Ready?"

Johnny answered, "Ready!"

The pitch was a fastball and it came right at him. Johnny, the right-hander, managed to leap back barely in time to avoid being hit. Otherwise, the ball might have torn into his left arm or shoulder. And this thing really would have been over.

"Throw strikes, you idiot!" Lefty angrily hollered out at the pitcher. "Let him hit the ball!"

Johnny suddenly felt just fine. He was no longer anxious. He was playing ball. The pitcher, a showboat like all pitchers, had tried to intimidate him.

He dug his cleats further into the dirt and stared back at the pitcher with a look that said, *Okay, buddy, now give me your best pitch. Give me something to hit—if you're up to it!*

And here it came again, this time a fastball down the center of the plate.

Johnny swung and connected solidly. The ball shot into the hole between left and center, a line drive that would have been at least a double in a game.

The next pitch he hit hard, but on the ground, two hops to right field.

Then another big drive that bounced off the chain-link fence in left.

The pitcher threw a curve. Johnny caught it squarely and whacked it to right.

Two more fastballs. Johnny swung and missed the first, fouled the other off to the left. Then he barely ticked a curve that bounced off the left field line.

The pitcher, always a pitcher, followed with a changeup, a slow pitch, hoping to catch this kid off stride and cause him to swing and miss.

But Johnny saw it coming, timed it perfectly, and crushed the ball. It sailed long and high over that center field green fence and, as they say on the radio, is probably still in the air somewhere out there in America.

"Okay, you can hit," said Lefty with a grin of real pleasure on his face. "Grab your glove and let's see if you can catch anything—besides a cold."

A player was told to start hitting fly balls to the kid out in center.

Johnny caught the first three easily. They were high pop-ups. Then came a couple of hard drives, one to Johnny's left, the other to the right. Johnny had no problem catching either. He made it look easy. As always.

What remained was something right at him. They are ordinarily the hardest for an outfielder to get a bead on.

Johnny took the first two, again, with ease, moving a few steps for one, a few to the rear for the other.

He knew what was coming, of course. Maybe not this time, but soon—eventually. There was going to be a hard line drive headed for the green fence behind him.

And here it was. As he had on that terrible night in Shepstown, he took off running almost with the *whack!* sound of the ball against the bat.

But this time he did take the quick glance to see where the fence was. And he stopped in time to stretch his left arm high for the ball, catching it securely in his glove and coming down gently with a soft, harmless bounce with his back against the green wood.

It was a move he had practiced fifty times, if not more, in his head in the weeks since his accident. This was the way to do it. This was the way he'd just *done* it.

And now, since tying the laces on his cleats, he had his first thought about his left arm. And the shoulder. Did they hurt? No. Had either—the arm or the shoulder—hurt at all while he'd been batting? No. While running? No.

Well, to be honest, there had been some quick shots of pain, some soreness. And, yes, some weakness, just what Dr. Mann had promised.

"Okay, kid, you're a Driver," said Lefty after Johnny responded to the manager's motion to come in from the outfield and join him behind home plate.

"Can I wear twenty-seven—Pete Reiser's number?" Johnny asked.

"It's all yours, kid."

ON TO WICHITA!

That was what it said in blue letters two feet high on a huge white canvas banner that was hung across the front of Mencken Field.

The first time Johnny saw it, he repeated the words out loud and threw a fist into the air. You bet, *on to Wichita*!

The Blue Ridge Drivers won their local league and took the district and the Maryland-Delaware state championships in quick order, winning each of the play-off series.

Their new center fielder had a lot to do with their end of the season surge. One story in the sports section of *The Baltimore Sun* called him "Pistol Johnny," saying he was cut from the same hitting and center fielder cloth as the great Pete Reiser. Some called him Johnny Oh. Next to the story was a large photo of Johnny in his batting stance. Nothing could have been finer for Johnny Wrigley.

He had a .374 batting average, hit fourteen home runs, knocked in a stunning forty-two runs total, and caught everything hit his way in center field. Lefty Oliphant had no trouble arranging for his new star to spend most of his days and nights laboring on behalf of Blue Ridge Motor Coaches on a baseball diamond rather than on the wash rack. That was fine with Johnny, of course, but he hadn't really minded that much getting the dirt and grime off those buses.

The "semi" in "semi-pro" meant ballplayers got paid, but not much. Most of their pay was known officially as expense money for equipment, meals, and other so-called essentials. For Johnny, it meant getting a fifty-dollar check every two weeks plus an occasional five-dollar bill from Lefty after he'd had a particularly outstanding game. It all added up to about what he'd been making on the cleaning crew.

The arm and shoulder held—mostly. He was careful, but he seldom favored or compensated so much that it kept him from doing what he needed to do at the plate and in the field—including going for the hard drives over his head against the green. Soreness and, occasionally, some swelling sometimes caused him to miss a game. He put ice on the arm and shoulder after every game. Once he talked Dr. Mann into giving him a shot of something to fight off a nagging pain that wouldn't go away.

He continued to go in regularly to see Dr. Mann, who not only cheered him on in his medical office as doctor to patient but came to several games and did it there, too. He was truly, to Johnny, a Miracle Whip god.

The yellow apple in the situation was that between playing ball and his treatments, there was absolutely no time for Rose—or any other girl.

NICK DIDDEN, THE *real* Blue Ridge driver, remained his savior and a man Johnny saw as a very special friend, the kind he'd never really had before, even in the marines. There had been people like Darwin for a moment, but then they were gone. *Dead* gone. Only their faces returned. That was the way of war friendships.

Johnny wanted to see and talk to Nick as often as possible, but Johnny's game and practice schedule and Nick's driving schedule didn't permit much of that.

Fortunately, it did work out for them to have a good-luck drink together the evening before Johnny and the Drivers were to leave on their morning special chartered Blue Ridge bus for Kansas. There was no game or practice for Johnny, and Nick had just finished his run from Pittsburgh. They met at the Dispatcher's, a small bar across the street from the downtown bus depot.

"You going to try for the pros again?" Nick asked Johnny after their first Jack Daniel's and a little how-you-been small talk.

"Dr. Mann thinks semi-pro may be all I'm ever going to be able to do," said Johnny. It was an honest answer. Everything he said to Nick was an honest answer.

"Go for it, Johnny. If you want it, go for it. There aren't a lot of second chances. You got one. Take it. Take it before it goes away."

Nick spoke those words gently, personally. His face suddenly flushed and also seemed to soften. This was not the normal demeanor of this military-mannered Blue Ridge bus operator.

Johnny almost said something. But he didn't.

And Nick continued.

"After Saipan while we were getting ready to hit Iwo Jima, our company commander came to me and said I'd been recommended for a battlefield commission. I was just a staff sergeant, but now, just like that, I would be a second lieutenant. An officer. He said I'd eventually be sent to officer's basic school at Quantico. I had already decided that I wanted to be a marine forever. A regular, a professional. When the war was over and everybody was discharged, I would stay in. I had even

thought—dreamed, really—that eventually I would be an officer. Now here it all was."

Nick looked out the bar window. There was a Greyhound
GMC Silversides coming out of the depot across the street.
NEW YORK was on its destination sign. "Now, that's a bus," Nick
said. "Better-looking than our ACFs or anything else we've got.
Trailways, too."

"Yeah," Johnny said. And he tensed while waiting for Nick
to pick up and finish his story. Johnny assumed it was going to
be a very bad finish. No surprise happy ending for Nick.

"I told the captain I accepted with great pleasure. He said
that I would be transferred immediately to the Second Division. The corps liked to have mustangs—you know, enlisted
who were made officers—start out fresh in new outfits. I told
him I'd rather wait then until after Iwo. I wanted to stay with
my people for that. So I did. And I was slammed by a Jap
rocket blast the third day after hitting the beach at Iwo. It blew
away a lung and a bunch of other stuff on my left side. I spent
seven months in the navy hospital in Philadelphia, was given a
medical discharge after being told I wasn't physically fit
enough to be a marine anymore—much less an officer. So here
I am commanding a bus again instead."

Johnny hurt for his special friend. And he definitely got the
obvious connection between Nick's story and his go! message.

But there was more to it than *Johnny, go!*

Johnny started talking. He told Nick about why "On to

Wichita!" was more than a baseball championship thing in his life. He knew it sounded crazy, but he couldn't help but dream that someday it would bring a particular girl out of wherever she was in Kansas. He described her, said her name was Betsy, told the story of the troop train and the several minutes at the Wichita train station. He skimmed over the details of what exactly had happened amidst the cigarettes and apples but said enough to make Johnny pretty sure Nick got it.

"I tried to find her right after the war, but I couldn't," Johnny said. Then he told of his day in Wichita, including his visit to Lawrence Stadium.

Nick's face had broken into a sympathetic smile that stayed in place until Johnny finished.

"Semper Fi and 'On to Wichita,' Johnny," he said then.

Johnny only smiled.

"Where were *you*?" Nick then asked. He said it abruptly, like a sudden smack on the face.

Johnny lost the smile, blinked his eyes, and moved his mouth to the ready position. It was going to happen. Here now he would, finally, for the first time ever, tell somebody about what had happened on Okinawa. And maybe, before that, Peleliu. Nick Didden had told Johnny his story. Now Johnny would tell Nick his.

Johnny licked his lips. Filled a second glass with whiskey. Sniffed. Glanced away and then back.

He threw down the Jack Daniel's barely taking a breath. And he said, "Okinawa. Oh-ki-nah-wah. If I had a snake, I'd name it that, Nick. Or a pet rat. Just saying the word makes my skin . . . Oh, I don't know what it makes my skin do. I was stupid enough to think nothing could be worse than Peleliu. On Peleliu, I saw so many dead bodies, ours and Japs. You probably did, too, on Saipan and Iwo. So many parts of bodies—ears, whole heads, arms, hands, even toes and fingers. I even came across some guy's nose once. I mean it. It was just lying there on one of those paths up a hill to a pillbox I was going to fill up with fire. Was it like that for you? I hope not, for your sake, Nick."

Nick said it was the same for him. Exactly the same.

Johnny had another whiskey. Then Nick started talking in detail about the new buses Greyhound had on the drawing boards to compete with Trailways and how Blue Ridge was trying to decide which kind to buy for themselves. The differences had more to do with looks than safety and sturdiness—at least that's what the drivers like Nick thought.

Soon Johnny said, in answer to no question:

"Oh-ki-nah-wah. They told us afterward it was the biggest and worst battle of the war—for the marines, at least. Maybe for everybody. Worse even than Peleliu. All I know is that I never in my life saw so many ships—ours, in our convoy. There were thousands of them. The Japs went after them with their suicide planes, the kamikaze. I watched from the deck of our LST while ten of them, maybe more, dove right into our big carriers and cruisers. Our folks got all excited about the Japs being so fanatical and stupid they'd fly a plane into something and kill themselves for the emperor. I never could figure out how that was any different from a U.S. marine running off an amtrack onto a beach being pretty damn sure he was going to die. Aren't they both suicide?"

Nick didn't respond. Instead, he quickly said it was already after eight o'clock, time to go, to quit the drinking as much as the talking.

"Watch that stuff, Johnny," Nick said, motioning to the glass of whiskey. "Got to be in top form for Wichita."

Johnny said he would watch that stuff.

"You're going to be fine, Johnny," Nick said as they exchanged goodbyes and good lucks.

JOHNNY WASN'T SO sure he was going to be fine. He wasn't sure what being fine even meant. Getting over Peleliu and Okinawa? Healing enough to make it back from the semi-pros to the pros?

Finding Betsy at the championships in Wichita?

Having too much whiskey certainly wasn't being fine.

Then, as he was walking very slowly down Pratt Street from the bar, he came to the Tivoli Theater, one of the largest and most lit up in downtown Baltimore.

ABILENE TOWN STARRING RANDOLPH SCOTT was on the marquee in huge letters. Johnny had already seen the movie with Rose.

But without a thought and for no conscious reason, Johnny bought a ticket for seventy-five cents at the box office and took a seat in the back of the darkened theater, where there were several empty seats.

In just a few seconds Johnny picked up the story enough to know that the movie was already more than half over.

Mr. Scott, playing the good-man town marshal, was trying to make peace between ranchers and cowboys from one side of Abilene and homesteaders and businessmen on the other side. Power, money, and women were on the line.

And after only a few pistols could be fired, fists thrown, girls grabbed, Johnny dozed off.

Johnny woke up after nine-thirty, when the lights came on at the end of the feature. He stood up and ambled back outside to the street toward where he lived, which was only twelve blocks away. There was a taste of dry awfulness in his mouth, and he still didn't believe he would be fine.

"Hey, Johnny Oh!"

It was a woman, with a man, leaning on a red pickup truck at the curb in front of Johnny's apartment house. The woman was Sylvia, his mother. The man was Stubby Hill, the Mack truck salesman from Shepstown.

Sylvia rushed over to meet Johnny and grabbed him around the neck. "It's dark and it's late and I couldn't find you anywhere," Sylvia said.

"I stopped for a drink . . . and a movie," Johnny said. "I didn't know you were coming anyhow."

"It was a surprise. Stubby here read in the paper that you

were leaving in the morning to play in the World Series," Sylvia said.

Johnny gave a frown toward Stubby, who said nothing. To hell with Stubby now and forever more, was pretty much Johnny's attitude.

Sylvia, oblivious to any of that, said, "I wanted to treat you to a big dinner of a grilled cheese and a French-fried turnip green—something fancy, Johnny Oh. Too late now."

"Sorry. It's not the real World Series, Mom. The semi-pro—"

"You've been drinking, haven't you?"

"I had a couple with an old bus driver friend. For good luck, you know."

Sylvia put her face right up to his mouth. "Breathe out," she said.

"I told you I'd had a drink or two," Johnny said.

"I was trying to see if you'd been chewing."

Johnny shook his head and laughed. "You are a real bunch of asparagus, you know that, Mom?"

"Better 'n being a box of barbecued Cracker Jacks. You going to write me a letter from Kansas? Tell me how it all went and everything?"

There had been no other letters from Baltimore after that first one. But Sylvia, sometimes with Stubby or by herself on the bus, had come to several of his Drivers games. They were in touch.

"Playing ball doesn't leave much time for writing letters,

Mom—please, you know that," Johnny said. "Like the war, re-member?"

Sylvia Wrigley hugged Johnny again. It was clearly a good-bye hug. It was almost ten o'clock, and she had to get back to Shepstown.

"Well, Good Humor bar luck in Kansas, or wherever you're going for the big games," she said. "And don't swallow any wooden gumdrops."

That was a new one for Johnny. And it made him laugh. His mom always made him laugh.

Sylvia climbed into the front seat of the red truck, as Stubby, not having said a word, scooted around to the driver's side.

"You ought to know, too, that Jeannie's getting married to that business math kid I told you about," Sylvia said.

Too bad, thought Johnny. But Jeannie wasn't anywhere near being on his mind at the moment.

"Whatever happened to that Rose girl you wrote about?" Sylvia asked, a parting question through the rolled-down win-dow.

Johnny just shook his head.

"You got a new girlfriend, Johnny Oh?"

Johnny nodded.

"She got a name?"

"Betsy," Johnny said.

JOHNNY SPENT VERY little of the next three days thinking about baseball or even the national semi-pro championship. Every moment of his waking time was centered on what exactly he was going to do when the bus arrived in Wichita. How he was going to go about finding Betsy, assuming she was still somewhere in Kansas to be found.

He could still bring her face back to the reflection in the bus window. His memories of the exact details of what had happened at the Wichita train station jumped back with full detail.

As he got closer and closer, his obsession with what he still saw as his Betsy luck got stronger and deeper, too. Yes, yes, it was definitely that luck that had led to the incredible miracle that had selected him to be allowed to live instead of Darwin and the lieutenant and all of the others, Okinawans and Japs included.

And it was that luck that had run out in center field at Shepstown.

Now maybe it would come back if he could only find her. . . .

Johnny, asking for an audience in the back of the bus just before it arrived in Wichita, laid one huge favor on Lefty Oliphant.

"Could you maybe see about getting my picture in the Wichita papers?" Johnny said. "I know it sounds showboaty, but I know somebody here in Kansas who I'd like to impress."

That whispered request turned out to be the sum total of Johnny's three days of thinking of a plan to find Betsy. It was based on the hope that somehow she would see the story, make the connection to the troop train, the apples and the cigarettes, the storeroom and the cot. Then, no matter where she now lived or in what situation—maybe even married or engaged, as was Jeannie with the light brown hair—Betsy with the curly bangs would rush madly to that Wichita stadium and throw herself and her future at Johnny Wrigley.

And life would be a chocolate éclair. Or a piece of apple pie à la mode.

Lefty managed to get done what Johnny wanted.

On the front page of the sports section of *The Wichita Eagle* the second morning after they got to town, there he was, the Blue Ridge Drivers' star center fielder, Johnny Wrigley. It was a large shot, two columns wide and maybe eight or more inches long. "The Baltimore Club's Top Slugger" was the headline over the photo.

Johnny was holding a bat in one hand and his uniform cap in the other, looking right at the camera. He had insisted that he not have his hat on when the picture was taken, the better for Betsy to see his face.

The brief story with the photo said: "This is actually Wrigley's second visit to Wichita. He was a marine in World War Two and he made a brief stopover at Union Station while traveling west on a troop train. 'They gave me cigarettes and apples,' he told the *Eagle*. 'And it was great.'"

The semi-pro national championship games worked on a system that Johnny didn't fully understand. What mattered was that twenty-four teams showed up from around the country and played day and night games among themselves for two weeks at that Lawrence Stadium in Wichita. The team with the best record at the end would be the winner.

Johnny's first game was against the Saint Joe Autos from Saint Joseph, Michigan.

He came onto the field before anyone else, hoping she might have come early to the ballpark. Real baseball fans do that to watch batting practice, infield and outfield warm-ups, wind sprints, and the other pregame rituals of baseball.

Johnny, of course, in his pre-Wichita daydreams on the bus, had already imagined it happening. She came down the concrete steps behind home plate, caught his eye, and gave him a wave and a gorgeous smile while beckoning him to join her down in front at the screen backstop behind home plate.

"Hello. I'm Betsy," she said.

"I know who you are," he said. "I'm Johnny."

"I know."

"I still love you."

"I love you, too," she said.

End of daydream.

His real Betsy was not among the early baseball fans to arrive that first evening. The stadium filled up with at least four thousand spectators, and he could not find her in the stands. He thought it didn't make sense that she would come and *not* find him—say something to him, if nothing else.

Forget the daydream! A single word or even just a smile to signal that you remembered Wichita would have been enough, Betsy.

That was a lie—to her and to himself. He wanted so much more than that to happen. He wanted Betsy luck and the rest of his life to happen.

Johnny had a weak night at the plate against the Autos, going one for three, his single in the fourth knocking in one run. His team lost 4–3. He had six major plays in the field, but nothing difficult beyond one drive to his left that he took on the run. The others were easy fly balls. During game two against Wichita's own Boeing Bombers, he went hitless, but the Blue Ridge Drivers won 2–1.

In the third game, Johnny hit a double in the eighth that knocked in two runs for the win. They won again when he went two for four in the fourth game, helping the Drivers stay very much alive—and in contention.

Each of the evenings, he scanned the crowd, and came up disappointed. Betsy had not come. Maybe she no longer lived in Kansas. Maybe she was still here but didn't read sports pages. Maybe she had seen the story about him and had seen his photograph and didn't care about him. Whatever it was, she wasn't there.

And she hadn't shown up for the fifth game—the awful one, his last one.

Johnny had trouble concentrating from the opening pitch of that game. His mind kept wandering off to Betsy, his few minutes with her, the rest of his real life without her, his imagined life with her—his Dear Betsys. He kept her face, her curly bangs, right there the way he remembered them from that afternoon. Could she have changed so much in just . . . how long had it been now? Still not quite three years? He felt strongly now that even from the stands or bleachers of this baseball stadium he would recognize that look about her that would shine through to him clearly—absolutely.

He was the Drivers' cleanup hitter batting fourth. On a 2-2 count he swung at and missed a breaking ball in the first inning, leaving a runner stranded. His second at bat, in the fourth, ended with his hitting a lame grounder to short. He did finally hit a double in the seventh to knock in a run. The Montgomery (Alabama) Acme Roofers were ahead 3 to 2 and time was running out.

And as he left the dugout to take his position in center for the eighth inning, Johnny again did his obsessive, nervous glance around both ways to the bleachers and the stands to see if she was there—maybe a late arrival?

He saw her! At least, *maybe* it was her. Yes, yes. That's her! Over there in the left field bleachers. She didn't have the bangs . . .

But he had to keep moving to his position, to take the field.

Once he got to his place in center, he focused intently on where he'd seen her. She was in about the third row up. Was that her waving at him right now? Oh, my God! Maybe it was her—even without the bangs.

He heard the crack of the bat against the ball.

Here it came, a hard drive. *Always,* a hard drive.

On the Wrigley-Reiser reflex, he turned and started running, keeping the ball in sight over his shoulder.

After several steps he knew—he just knew—he was coming up on the fence. He moved his head slightly to see where he was. Yes, it was right there! He turned back and, for a panicky hair of a second, couldn't see the ball!

But there it was. Still coming high and fast. He sprung up with both legs, using every ounce of energy he had, his mitt as high over his head as his weakened arm and shoulder would permit.

He misjudged the leap—slightly. The ball was just inches out of reach. It smacked against the fence. He was still in the

JIM LEHRER

air—moving. He desperately tried to twist his body so his good right arm and side would break his fall. . . .

Too late. His bad left arm and shoulder crashed hard into the green fence.

PLAYERS AND COACHES helped him up to his feet and into the dugout. He could walk. But he was hurting. He had no idea how much havoc had been done to that already damaged shoulder and arm. He had no idea about anything.

A Wichita doctor who attended the games came with him to the players' dressing room. He said an ambulance was standing by if he needed to go to the hospital. He asked Johnny to lie down on a trainer's table so he could take a look.

And in a few minutes, the doctor told Johnny a young girl had come to see him and wanted some private moments with him. He said it was all right with him if it was with Johnny.

Johnny moved his head slightly.

"You're Johnny, the marine on the troop train, aren't you?"

Johnny didn't even have to look to know that this was the voice of his Betsy.

She came so close he could smell her. She was so close he could feel her. There was so much to say, to do.

"Betsy?" he said.

"Janet. My name is Janet." She said it sternly. Peculiarly so, it seemed to Johnny. But it was definitely *her* voice. Betsy's voice.

"Betsy?" Johnny said again.

· 192 ·

She said: "Janet. I may have used another name—like Betsy, possibly—at the Wichita train station. We did that sometimes. I lived in Hillsdale, Kansas. Our group came from there and other towns around."

"Lehighton," Johnny said. "I went to a town called Lehighton looking for you."

"I wasn't there," she said.

"I know," he said.

Something was different about her.

Her bang-less blond hair was combed tight straight back from her forehead and rolled up in an old-fashioned bun on the back of her head. That was the way some of the Amish around western Maryland wore it. And her solid gray dress was long-sleeved, and the full pleated skirt was almost to her ankles. She wore heavy off-white stockings and black shoes with large strings and wide stubby heels. There was not even a hint of makeup on her face.

Something was not right.

His Betsy in the storeroom had said she was religious. But not like *this*. What kind of church had she said she went to? Something named after some guy named Heinrich? She had talked on and on and on about it. Could she have gotten even more religious in the last three years? Had the war done something to her? Or had what they'd done in the storeroom done something to her?

Everything was different.

She also seemed heavier. Or was it the way she was dressed? She had seemed before so perfectly proportioned, so . . . well, stacked, to put it straight. Of course, he had been with her for only a few minutes on that train station cot, and she had been fully clothed—pretty much—all of the time.

Everything was not right.

Those dark eyes certainly matched, almost perfectly. More than almost. So did the warm, welcoming, special look on her slightly wider face.

But this was nobody Johnny Oh Wrigley knew or had ever seen before.

"How was the awful war for you?" she asked.

"The war was fine, no problems," he said. "I loved every minute of it."

He wanted very much not to be there with her any longer.

"Did you end up going overseas?" the girl asked.

Johnny shook his head. He wished he'd been knocked out cold at this Kansas ballpark as he had at Shepstown.

She, Janet, said: "My husband, Jacob, was a conscientious objector who participated in a starvation experiment in Minnesota instead of the military. He served his country with courage and distinction."

Johnny just closed his eyes.

"What did you do in the marines?" she asked.

"I just played baseball," Johnny said, his eyes still closed.

"I heard the marines were the worst of the killers," she said. "You should feel free to ask for forgiveness."

The pain in Johnny's arm and shoulder were now spreading through every part of his body, including down into his stomach and up into his head—and even into his haunted heart. Everything in him hurt.

"Jacob and I are studying conflict and forgiveness as powers for good and evil," said the girl, Janet. "Are you aware of the writings of Hutchinson and Kingman?"

Johnny shook his head. Hutchinson and Kingman? They could have been minor-league third basemen or towns in Kansas, for all he knew.

"Jacob was one of thirty-six volunteers in the Minnesota starvation project," said the girl. "Jacob went from weighing 162.7 pounds to 112.3 pounds. The point was to study the effects of starvation in order to have the data needed to help those poor souls recovering from the war effects of prison and concentration camps. . . ."

Johnny, in a way he'd never known was possible before, now closed his ears along with his eyes.

The girl who called herself Janet was still talking and talking. Johnny could hear the sound of her voice but could not make out her words.

Then after a while, he noticed the noise had ended. The girl wasn't talking anymore.

So he opened his eyes and ears again.

And before he could close them back, the girl said, "Well, you should know that I have made my peace with God and Jacob about what happened that afternoon at the train station." She briefly closed *her* eyes and put her hands together as if praying, just as she had done that afternoon among the smokes and apples.

"So as long as you put your hands together and say you're sorry, anything goes?" Johnny said. "That's how it works?"

Her face seemed to flush ever so slightly. "I have forgiven you, too, for what you did to me," she said quickly. "You can rest assured that there were no physical or mental as well as moral consequences from what happened."

Johnny knew what that meant. That those few moments on the cot had not made her pregnant. "I did nothing to you," said Johnny. "I wasn't there."

"You weren't there? I was so certain it was you. I spoke to both God in heaven on my knees and to Jacob about you and what we had done—you and I. I also told my aunt Lena, who was with me that afternoon."

Johnny looked away. *Why did you tell some Aunt Lena? I never told anybody. Except Darwin. And he's dead.*

She said, "Aunt Lena showed me the picture of you in the newspaper. The story said you had stopped on a troop train at Wichita during the war and now you were a baseball player representing a team from Maryland. That is why I came here tonight. Lena came with me on the bus, which was late. Johnny was the name in the paper. Johnny was the name of the marine I remember. He had freckles, too, as you do. I was certain it was you."

Johnny felt the need to escape from his pain and suffering—his present. "They got everything wrong," he said.

You are not my Betsy!

"They got everything wrong," he repeated as he tried now to will himself out cold before he started screaming.

"Are you absolutely sure you're not the one who threw a yellow apple out into the traffic?"

"You are not my Betsy, goddamn it!" Johnny screamed, causing the girl, Janet, to blanch and to race quickly out of the locker room.

JOHNNY COULDN'T REMEMBER much of anything about the trip to Baltimore. The Drivers did not win the national semi-pro championship. They rode back on the same Blue Ridge bus—a war-weary ACF Brill—straight through from Wichita via Saint Louis, Columbus, and Pittsburgh, with the two real Blue Ridge drivers on board switching off driving.

There was little talk and absolutely no joy among the Drivers. They did get an hour-long rest stop in Saint Louis and another in Pittsburgh, which Johnny spent all but a few minutes of by himself, shuffling around the cities like a sick old man, or sitting away from everyone on one of the high-backed wooden benches in a far corner of a Greyhound bus station. He welcomed the break from his teammates, from the camaraderie of their shared defeat—and his own special sadness.

Johnny did everything humanly possibly to keep away

thoughts about the girl who'd said her real name was Janet. He longed to erase her from his mind the way a good washing would clean a blackboard. Eliminate forever the sight of her—the stranger—back there in the locker room. *Stranger?*

Someday he would think about all of this, consider seriously what he'd said to the girl, the one who'd said she was Janet, the one who had brought him Betsy luck at Peleliu and Okinawa. He wasn't sure yet what he had really done about her. Or why.

The only thing Johnny wished right now was that maybe one of those real Blue Ridge drivers would steer this bus off a bridge—or a cliff.

He'd seen himself dead hundreds of times in daydreams, including a few with him at Methodist funerals organized by his mother. And he had imagined seeing his body in movies and in O. Henry's stories, such as "The Furnished Room," which ended with people dying. Not to mention the real thing so many times in the war. Johnny still often marveled at the fact that he himself wasn't dead. He'd figured since the day he'd enlisted in the marines that some Jap might kill him. He'd told the Kansas girl—Betsy, or whoever. *Betsy!* Sure, he'd been trying to make her feel sorry for him that afternoon in the storeroom. But there had been some truth to it. He'd never thought of doing it to himself. Although, as he'd told Nick, there were times on Peleliu and Okinawa when what he was doing was probably about as close to suicide as you could get. That was different. That was what marines did. Particularly kid lieutenants and kid flamethrower operators.

Much of what he was experiencing during the Wichita-to-Baltimore trip was physical pain. A doctor at a hospital in Wichita had given him some pills to take on the trip. "But it's still going to hurt like heck every time the bus stops, turns, or even goes over a bump," said the doctor. Like heck? Heck. That silly word was just more of what the girl—*Betsy!*—had said before. Kansas people don't lie and they don't drink and they probably don't even say "hell." They say "heck."

The heck doctor was right, though. That re-torn-up arm and shoulder never stopped hurting from the time Johnny ran into that Wichita fence. Nothing much had gotten better since he'd lain there on the outfield grass, waiting for something to happen next, with the very real possibility there might be no more nexts.

Johnny thought about the guy in "The Furnished Room" who couldn't find his lost girlfriend. The Japs should have gotten Johnny anyhow. That *had* to have been God's real plan for him. Maybe the Betsy luck and the Miracle Whips that had kept him alive on amtracks and beaches and in craters and fox-holes had all been mistakes. They were accidents—misreadings of what God had really had in mind. Erase them from the black-board. Goodbye from Oh Johnny Oh Wrigley.

There were other things always racing through his mind. The sights of what remained of Anderson, Darwin, and that kid lieutenant and so many other kid marines who hadn't gotten any luck or miracles.

And the horrifying sights of what he'd done with a flamethrower.

———

NOW, BACK IN Baltimore, here again was Dr. Mann, the miracle man himself, confirming the worst of the worst.

"Write 'em off, Johnny," said the doctor.

He was talking about Johnny's left arm and shoulder after an examination at that Johns Hopkins hospital.

"Forget baseball. Anything that requires any serious use of the full upper left part of your body is no more."

"What about lifting a glass of Jack Daniel's?" Johnny said.

"Refresh my memory, Johnny," said Mann. "How old are you right now—at this very moment?"

Johnny actually had to think about it for a second or two. Birthdays had always been big deals with him and his mom, but not after what he'd seen and done as a marine.

"Twenty," Johnny said finally. "I'm twenty years old."

"And life is over for you because you can't play a game called baseball anymore because you misjudged a fly ball to center and cracked up an arm and shoulder again?" said the doctor. "That's whining bullshit, Johnny."

Johnny was sitting in a chair across from a desk in a tiny office on the sixth floor next to an examination room. He wanted some Jack Daniel's.

Mann, the tough former army combat doctor, kept talking to him like he was his commanding officer, not his physician.

"What are you going to do with yourself, Johnny?"

Johnny just shook his head. He had no answer to that. He

had avoided even thinking about it during and since those three awful days on the bus.

"One option *is* to be a drunk," Mann said. "Spend a lot of time crying with your friend Jack Daniel's every day. You can do that until your money runs out. Then they'll put you in a stinking fleabag poorhouse somewhere in south Baltimore. The Salvation Army's already got a thriving business dealing with guys who couldn't move on past what happened to them in the war. Some people call it shell shock."

"I'd call it flame shock," Johnny mumbled.

Jerry Mann kept talking, but Johnny wasn't listening. Johnny thought this kind of crap was like watching a big rock rolling down a hill right at you. Here it comes. It's too big for you to stop it, too late to run away from it, so let it roll. Let it smash you into smithereens.

He almost whined. He almost told the doctor that he had fallen in love like a rock with the most beautiful, most marvelous, most perfect girl in the world. But the fall was over. Because of what she looked like now. What she said—now. He no longer saw her as beautiful or marvelous or perfect. He saw her as somebody else—somebody he didn't know. And definitely didn't love, didn't want to spend his life with. That girl had disappeared.

"Listen to me, goddamn it!" Mann yelled.

Johnny Wrigley stood up, picked up a water glass from the desk in front of Dr. Mann. It was two-thirds full of water.

"Watch this, goddamn it!" Johnny yelled back. And he tossed the water into the face of the doctor.

Mann didn't react. He didn't even make an attempt to wipe the water off his face or desk.

"Now listen to *me*, goddamn it," Johnny said in a trembling quiet voice that was nothing like a yell.

He sat back down. And talked. Finally, he talked about what really mattered.

"Every once in a while they'd come around and tell people they were being put in for a medal for something they'd done. That happened to me on Okinawa. A sergeant told me I was going to get a Silver Star for what I'd done. I yelled at him that I didn't want a goddamn medal for what I'd done. He thought I was crazy, and he'd probably have had me tied up and sent to a corpsman or a doctor like you if somebody hadn't needed me and my fire machine again right away. On Okinawa, they always needed me and my flames to kill somebody. They gave me a new one to replace mine that blew up with a guy named Darwin on Peleliu."

Dr. Mann raised his right hand as if he were a traffic cop. "You okay, Johnny? You don't have to do this. To say anything more about all of this. You want to keep talking?"

Yeah, he wanted to keep talking.

"Some Jap soldiers had taken a bunch of Okinawan civilians into a cave with them. It was a huge cave, one of thousands all over that island. But our people didn't see the civilians—or, at least, didn't tell me about them. All they told me was 'Do your thing, Wrigley. Burn the little bastards out of there.' They pointed up ahead a hundred yards or so at a cave opening. All I saw was the opening, about the size of a one-car-garage door.

"Some riflemen covered me as I made my way up there to get me and my new machine in range. I got into position, the assistant operator did his thing, and then I shot off two bursts from my machine. I was, as usual, right on target. I was good, Doctor. Really good. That stream of fire went right through the opening. 'Bull's-eye!' yelled the assistant. 'I can smell 'em burning.'

"We both started running—you know, the way flamethrower people who want to stay alive do after firing. But we stopped. Because we saw people coming out of that cave. Because the first to come were three Okinawan kids. Little ones. Not more than three or four years old. They were in flame from head to foot. That's who we were smelling. Then came two women. Probably the mothers of the kids. That's who we were smelling. And four more children. That's who we were smelling. More kids and more women. I didn't count. I couldn't count. All were burning, and they were screaming and crying—and smelling. They had all been covered by my liquid flames, just like you were just now with that water from that glass."

Now Dr. Mann grabbed a cloth handkerchief and, finally, wiped the wetness from his face and head. But he said nothing. He was still listening.

Johnny said: "My flame shock is the sound from those kids.

It went through my ears, down inside me somewhere, and wouldn't come out and go away. It still hasn't, doctor. There is no medal, no Miracle Whip that ever will make it go away."

"It's got to, Johnny," said the doctor. "It's just got to."

"Got to." What in the hell does that mean?

He stood up and thought for a flash of a second about picking up the doctor's DiMaggio ball. But he didn't.

JOHNNY SAW THE large padlocks on the main public gates, but he knew there was always a small side gate for players that was never pushed in all the way. That was just in case a Driver sometime felt the private need to sweat, to practice sliding, to throw a few or hit a few.

There wasn't anybody out there doing any of that now, of course. The baseball season for Mencken Field and the Drivers was over. Way, way over.

And it was getting dark. But there was more than enough light for Johnny to see everything he needed to see. The ticket offices outside the main entrance, the locked-up vacant concession booths behind the grandstands, the concrete steps up to the rows of the dark blue wooden seats behind, and on either side of home plate, the team dugouts, the uncovered bleachers off to both sides.

Johnny stepped up on the top of the home team dugout on the left side and, using his one good arm, gently dropped himself down onto the ground—to the field of play.

The infield dirt was not raked. There were potholes from rain. The infield grass was ragged. And he could see the out-field grass was in bad shape, too. There were no bases out, of course, and home plate needed a brushing off and some white-wash painting, as did the pitcher's mound. Both were made of wood. The white chalk lines along the first and third foul lines had long ago been rubbed out.

Johnny stood at the pitcher's mound. He turned from one side to the other, and around back to home plate and then to the outfield fences. This was a baseball field. Even in the dark, he had no trouble seeing exactly what this place would look like in the spring—early April—when Mencken Field was made ready again for another season of baseball. All of the rak-ing and the mowing and the painting and the fixing would be done. This was a place where the game of baseball was played.

Johnny faced center field and said out loud in a normal voice:

Dear Betsy,

It's me again. It's been a while, I know. How's it been going for you? The singing working well? I bet it is. I hope you've been singing a lot. 'Haunted Heart' is still my fa-vorite. I never did remember for sure if it was Dinah Shore who made it really famous. Somebody said it may have been Jo Stafford. I don't know much about her singing. I'm really doing well in baseball. I don't want to brag but I made it quickly and easily to the Dallas Rebels and then on to the

Detroit Tigers. I'm the starting center fielder for the Tigers. That's the big leagues—the majors. They're comparing me to Pistol Pete already. I hit a double in the top of the ninth against the A's last night. Knocked in the winning run. Also made five putouts in center—two of them hard plays that I had to run for. As they say, I made 'em look easy. My batting average is just under .300, which is great. No errors yet at center. Fingers crossed. Stolen a few bases. Baseball's working for me, that's the important thing. I knew it would. That's my life. But, now that I think about it, I can't go until I tell you I still can hardly wait to see what our kids are going to look like. I'll bet the girls will be beautiful, bangs and all, like their mother, and the boys will be center fielders like their dad. Maybe shortstops. That's a tough position, having to go for grounders both to the right and the left and throw while still moving. We're headed to New York tonight for a doubleheader tomorrow against the Yankees. I still get a thrill just playing in a game with Joltin' Joe DiMaggio. I may ask Joe to autograph a ball for me. I still haven't gotten an autograph for Pistol Pete. We never play against each other because the Dodgers are in the National League and we're in the American. Remember what I always tell you. I love you. I loved you from the first magic second I saw you on that Kansas train platform, and I always will love you. I can see your face the way it was then, and I always will.

> *With my love always,*
> *Johnny Oh*

Johnny thought about adding something about the man in O. Henry's story about the dream. Or the Christmas one about the couple with the hair and the watch. He even thought about making up a short story of his own. Maybe about a ballplayer who thought he was Pete Reiser but wasn't.

He was still standing on the pitcher's mound. He yanked a pint bottle of Jack Daniel's from a pocket, took a long swallow from it, tossed the bottle to the side.

And broke into the great wide smile of a happy man.

Then he pulled out a letter-size envelope and set it down carefully on the ground.

He shook his shoulders, including the ruined one, as if he were getting ready to take the field. That's what he always did. Even in high school, that's what he did before he ran off toward center. He shook his shoulders in a way of signaling to one and all, *Here I come!*

He took off running as fast as he could toward the green in the middle of the center field fence at Mencken.

With his eyes wide open, still grinning, he crashed at full speed into the green wood.

It hurt. It stunned. He fell straight back onto the ground, onto the untrimmed grass of center field.

Within seconds, he was up on his feet again. He moved slowly back from the fence about halfway to the pitcher's mound.

He took off running again as hard and as fast as he could.

And again he slammed with a huge bang right into the

fence. That almost did it. Johnny lay there for a while until he came to, until his eyes slowly crept open one more time.

His head hurt like hell. So did both of his shoulders and arms, the good and the bad. There was aching in his knees and even his stomach. And heart. Blood was dripping out of his nose; one of his eyes was closing.

But after a while he could still get up. He could still move.

So for the third time he made his way back to a starting position in front of the green part of the center field fence.

He gave it one more big smile for his Betsy, and with a power and strength way beyond what his first two crashings should have permitted, he lit out again for the green as fast as he could run.

But he stopped running. Suddenly. Like he had slammed on some brakes. He walked a few steps. And then he stood absolutely still. The fence was still five yards away.

Johnny Wrigley sat down on the outfield grass, crossed his legs in front of him, dropped his head into his arms, and cried.

The tears came gushing out between the lids of Johnny's eyes the way his mom had said they should.

Like the water in Antietam Creek coming down from the mountains when the snow melts in the spring.

"MY GOD, YOU look a mess, kid," said somebody. It was a grown man's voice. Johnny could hear it but not recognize it.

Johnny, his face still wet, didn't look up to see if he recognized the man himself.

"I live across the street and heard that banging into the fence . . . came out and found you here," said the man who was talking. "How in the hell did this happen?"

Johnny shrugged.

"Are you hurt?" asked the man.

Johnny felt an awful humming pain everywhere in his body. But it was going away. Finally.

The pain was going away!

"Try to move something—anything," said the man.

Johnny made the effort to move something—anything. He raised his right hand. His throwing hand.

"You run into that fence? How in the hell did that happen?"

Johnny didn't want to answer the man. He didn't want to say he'd run into that fence on purpose. But only two times. He stopped before the third.

"You need some help? An ambulance?" said the man.

Johnny shook his head. He didn't need any help. An ambulance.

"Okay then, kid. Take care of yourself."

Johnny could hear the sound of footsteps in the outfield grass.

Then, suddenly that noise stopped. And then came running sounds back toward Johnny, who could now see pretty clearly despite the hits and the dark.

"Can you feel this?" the man asked.

Johnny felt something down in the palm of his throwing

hand. He could feel the threads on the seams and the smoothness of the horsehide.

It was a baseball.

"I found this old ball just lying there out near the infield— scuffed and dirty," said the man. "Somebody must have forgotten to pick it up when the season ended."

Johnny slowly moved the fingers of his right hand around the ball. A faded blue *D* for Drivers was painted on it, which meant it was used only for batting practice.

And Johnny tightened the grip on that ball as hard as he could.

"Goodbye, Betsy," he said aloud, his head now raised up and away.

"Hey, I also found this by the pitcher's mound," the man said, handing Johnny a letter-size envelope. "It's got 'Sylvia Wrigley' written on it, not Betsy. Is it yours?"

Johnny nodded, took the letter, and stuffed it back into a pocket.

Epilogue

JOHNNY WENT BACK to work at the Blue Ridge Motor Coaches garage. He became a bus cleaner because he was no longer physically able to do what was required on the wash rack. His new duties involved using a broom and a big paper trash bag to collect cigarette butts, chewing gum, uneaten food, wet tissues, and other items of trash left by passengers—some of it downright disgusting.

His luck changed dramatically one day when he was sent off to ride an empty bus from the garage to the depot. A sweep-up job on a turnaround bus that was running late was needed—on the double. While waiting for a ride back afterward, Johnny ran into Harry Greenleaf, the Blue Ridge chief passenger traffic manager. Johnny had met him a time or two around the garage and at a company picnic. Mr. Greenleaf was a big baseball fan and supporter of the Drivers.

Mr. Greenleaf said, "Sorry about what happened in Wichita, Johnny. You were some ballplayer. Arm and shoulder going to be okay?"

Johnny nodded as he instinctually moved his right hand around to touch his left arm. The steady pain was diminishing, but the arm had no strength. There never would be much. Mr. Greenleaf then asked Johnny if he'd be interested in switching to another kind of job with the company—something at the depot?

That led to Johnny's becoming a ticket agent, a job that he enjoyed from the very beginning. He was issued a sharp uniform of dark blue gabardine trousers, a light blue dress shirt, and a dark blue tie. That made him feel official. Almost like he had at Parris Island when he'd first dressed up as a marine.

The work required no serious lifting or reaching, so it was no strain physically. His greatest pleasure was calling the buses over the public address system—yelling out the names of all the towns and the connections to and between New York and Boston to the north; Washington, Richmond, and Florida to the south; and to Pittsburgh, Columbus, Saint Louis, Chicago, and everywhere else as far west as Los Angeles and San Francisco. He finished every station call by telling the passengers to please not forget their baggage and by thanking them for riding the bus—for "seeing America at the scenery level."

Johnny thoroughly enjoyed talking to most everyone who came around the terminal—other agents, drivers, porters, baggage checkers, lunchroom waitresses, and cooks as well as passengers. The place was full of characters who Johnny believed would be a good fit in almost any O. Henry story.

Not all of them were fun. There were drunks and bums who kept Johnny constantly reminded of his own possibilities. Several were veterans with shocked looks in their eyes. Johnny could tell that they were still off somewhere in a nightmare of flying body parts, burning skin, bleeding gashes, horrifying screams, shaking sobs.

Johnny kept baseball in his life. Lefty Oliphant agreed to let Johnny continue to wear his number twenty-seven Drivers uniform and do some occasional third-base coaching and batting instruction. Johnny spent as much time with the players, particularly the young ones, as his depot work schedule would permit until the team was disbanded in 1962. That's when Blue Ridge Motor Coaches became part of Greyhound lines, which was not interested in fielding a semi-pro baseball team.

Johnny stayed on with Greyhound, continuing as a ticket agent until promoted to assistant district passenger agent. That was a traveling job that involved servicing the needs of the small depots and commission agents throughout Maryland, Delaware, and parts of West Virginia and Pennsylvania.

Johnny reached the Greyhound forced retirement age in 1990. He spent much of his time being an avid fan of the American League Baltimore Orioles and reading books, mostly novels and short stories by Ernest Hemingway, Jack London, and John Steinbeck as well as O. Henry and others. That reading interest flowed from several night college classes on American writing that he took through the years. His wife, Rose, had gone on to become the office manager of a medium-size law firm in Baltimore. She had two miscarriages that resulted in surgery that prevented her from having children. She and Johnny kept working until their respective retirements.

Rose had been a heavy smoker and she died of lung cancer at age sixty-eight. Jeannie Allen Jackson, who with the assistance of regular dye jobs still had light brown hair, reentered Johnny's life. Jeannie was a widow when she and Johnny happened to move into the same assisted living facility in Shepstown. They developed a warm personal relationship that provided both companionship and pleasure until Johnny's death.

Johnny died from a serious form of asthma that, even with a variety of oxygen tanks, masks, and other equipment, eventually made breathing impossible.

Some of the old Greyhound/Blue Ridge and baseball people made sure there was this obituary in *The Baltimore Sun* about Johnny:

Johnny Wrigley, a longtime area baseball player and bus company employee, died Wednesday at the Piedmont Memorial Living Center in Shepstown. He was eighty-two years old and suffered from a respiratory ailment.

Mr. Wrigley was a standout center fielder for Lafayette High School in the 1940s and played during one season for the Class B Shepstown Bobcats, a Detroit Tigers farm team in the Interstate League. Later he starred for the Blue Ridge Drivers, a semi-pro team that made it to the 1946 world championship series in Wichita, Kansas.

Mr. Wrigley served in the Pacific with the marines in World War Two.

He had no immediate survivors. His wife, the former Rose DeCarlo, preceded him in death. Sylvia Wrigley, Mr. Wrigley's mother, had managed the Red Rooster, a popular Shepstown grocery store, for many years. She died in 1981.

While not mentioned in the obit, three other important people in Johnny's life also passed away before he did. Nick Didden's internal wounds from Iwo Jima led eventually to a kidney problem that couldn't be repaired. Dr. Jerry Mann lost his life flying his own four-seater Cessna when it crashed on takeoff from a small airport north of Baltimore in heavy rain. Pistol Pete Reiser died of emphysema in Palm Springs, California, at age sixty-two. He and Johnny never met.

Jeannie Allen saw to the funeral arrangements for Johnny, although there was not that much to do. He had prepaid a funeral home for a casket, a small service, and a burial plot in Lafayette. The marine recruiting office in Baltimore, after checking Johnny's official combat record, readily agreed to send a four-man honor guard in dress blues. That and a couple of songs he wanted sung were all that Johnny had asked the undertaker to arrange.

While going through Johnny's few personal effects, Jeannie

came across a small black leather-covered case with the words
"Silver Star Medal" inscribed in gold leaf on the top. There was
a single sheet of official stationery folded underneath that de-
tailed what "John Charles Wrigley, PFC, USMC," had done
on the island of Okinawa in 1945. They said "with great risk to
his own safety" Johnny had "used his extraordinary skills as a
flamethrower operator to fend off a savage onslaught by the
enemy forces of the Japanese." His "conspicuous gallantry and
intrepidity in action" were described as being in "the highest
traditions of the marine corps and the United States naval
service."

Jeannie also found an old letter-size envelope that had
never been mailed.

"Sylvia Wrigley" was handwritten on the front of the envelope in a loopy penmanship that Jeannie was sure at a glance
was Johnny's. There was no address. The envelope, wrinkled
and brittle, was not sealed.

Jeannie felt comfortable reading what Johnny had written.

Dear Mom,

*So here is letter number thirteen. There were those
eleven from the war and then number twelve from Baltimore and now this one. Thirteen means bad luck, and that
sure fits. I've had it, Mom. My luck held while I was in the
marines, but it ran out. I can't be a ballplayer, not even a
small-time one, and I don't know what else to do with myself. I decided I really was intended to die in the war in-*

stead of Mickey. Something or somebody screwed up the plan. So I'm going to go ahead and stay with the original plan. Please don't let this upset you too much. You were the best mom anybody in the world could ever have. Apple pie à la mode and chocolate éclair and everything else good there could be. I know you wanted me to be something more than a ballplayer. I hope you don't think I let you down in a Crisco lard way. I love you, Mom.

Cock-a-doodle-doo forever,
Johnny Oh

Jeannie left the letter and the medal at the funeral home to be put in the casket with Johnny's body.

The undertaker, also at Jeannie's request, tossed in a baseball that Johnny had kept on his nightstand. He called it his "luck charm for life." The ball was scuffed and dirty and had a faded letter *D* painted on it in blue.

At the graveside service, presided over by a Methodist minister, the four marines joined with Jeannie and a couple dozen other folks from the center in singing "The Marines' Hymn" and "Bringing in the Sheaves."

Acknowledgments

I had much help. I talked through the initial idea first with my son-in-law, Lew Nash. Sarah Kaufman gave me a guided tour of the old Union Station building in Wichita, the home to Cox Cable. Michele Enke, the local history librarian at the Wichita Public Library, helped me find city directories, among other valuable items. The basis for everything I wrote about the battle of Peleliu came from Bill Sloan's terrific book, *Brotherhood of Heroes*. (It is a happy coincidence that Bill and I worked as reporters together at the Dallas *Times Herald* in the 1960s.) I also want to thank my assistant Roma Hare for some music advice, and the good people at Old Town Martini, a Wichita restaurant, for a table at which to labor—and observe.

This book is dedicated to Bob Loomis, my editor at Random House. That's because without him it would never have happened.

PHOTO © DON PERDUE

This is JIM LEHRER's nineteenth novel. He is also the author of two memoirs and three plays and is the executive editor and anchor of *The NewsHour with Jim Lehrer* on PBS. He lives in Washington, D.C., with his novelist wife, Kate. They have three daughters.

ABOUT THE TYPE

This book was set in Fairfield, the first typeface from the hand of the distinguished American artist and engraver Rudolph Ruzicka (1883–1978). In its structure, Fairfield displays the sober and sane qualities of the master craftsman whose talent has long been dedicated to clarity. It is this trait that accounts for the trim grace and vigor, the spirited design, and sensitive balance of this original typeface.

Rudolph Ruzicka was born in Bohemia and came to America in 1894. He set up his own shop, devoted to wood engraving and printing, in New York in 1913, after a varied career working as a wood engraver, in photoengraving and banknote-printing plants, and as an art director and freelance artist. He designed and illustrated many books, and was the creator of a considerable list of individual prints—wood engravings, line engravings on copper, and aquatints.